The Ones That I Hold Dear

Charvella J. Campbell

ICENI
BooKS

The Ones That I Hold Dear

Copyright © 2004 Charvella J. Campbell

Published by Iceni Books™
610 East Delano Street, Suite 104
Tucson, Arizona 85705

ISBN: 1-58736-246-5
LCCN: 2003110763

Throughout our journey of life we come across people that can have either a positive or negative impact on us. Friends even come and go... Nevertheless, the oldest yet strongest foundation in our society is the family. We may not always get along or understand one another. Sometimes we even choose estrangement as a solution to our family conflicts. Time after time, most of us realize that this only causes more distance, bitterness and hurt feelings.

Family is the core of our community; therefore, we should draw comfort from our mothers, guidance from our fathers, loyalty from our spouses, and joy from our children. Despite our differences, love should be the prevailing force that holds a family together. With unity and loyalty through tough times, we really have the opportunity to see just what our family can be. We get to examine its substance, and last but not least, our family bond can make us better people.

The following story focuses on the strong-willed yet compassionate matriarch of a family and her adult children. Through challenging times she serves as their anchor. In turn, she allows them to uplift her as well.

I hope that you will take away something special from this work and allow it to affect your own life in a positive light. Embrace the meaning of your own family and live it every day...

Mrs. Marguerite Glover wakes up one Saturday morning and begins her day. She has been retired now for almost a year, formerly being an elementary school teacher. Mrs. Glover is the widow of Charles Glover who passed away ten years earlier due to heart failure. Losing her beloved Charles was a blow to Mrs. Glover, and she deliberately kept teaching just to keep herself busy. She could have retired much sooner. Finally, one of her sons tried to convince her to do so. Her reply: "What am I going to do in that big ol' house by myself? Just sit there all day and look at Charles's pictures or watch TV until I go blind? I need to keep teaching. There's nothing else left for me to do."

Despite this remark, Mrs. Glover did retire eventually. She started focusing more on doing positive things with her time instead of feeling useless. In addition, she knew that her children and grandchildren would rally around her on a frequent basis. She would always have plenty of love and support.

Keith Glover is the oldest of four. He is a 45-year-old family man. Keith is married to Cassandra Eubanks-Glover, a claims adjuster for an insurance company. They have three children:

Chavonne, 17; Michael, 15; and Kyla, 12. Rough times have hit Keith's family recently. Not too long ago, he was laid off from his supervisory position at a factory. As technology and other factors changed, the company started downsizing; unfortunately, Keith was one of the victims. He had been working with machinery for over ten years and was quite skilled. Not for one moment did Keith ever think that the company would do such a thing to him after all of his dedication and hard work. He felt embittered and betrayed.

After searching for months to find decent employment, Keith settled for a job as a toll collector. He stood in a tollbooth all day long handing out tickets and nodding his head to people as they drove by in their cars. The pay cut greatly affected the family budget. Fortunately, Keith's wife Cassandra had a good-paying job that certainly contributed to the family's financial situation. He realized that no matter how hard it seemed, he was not alone. He had her support.

Gerard Glover is the black sheep of the family. He could be most fittingly described as a hustler up to no good. He is a 42-year-old man who is always out to get a quick buck but never willing to work hard at anything. He has spent his whole life in trouble with the law or dodging loan sharks or street lowlifes. Gerard's relationship with his immediate family is strained; however, he and Keith seem to be the most complicated. The two men are not only brothers but were also best friends when they were children. Years of bitter arguments and even a few shoves and pushes here and there have completely deteriorated their close bond—not to mention Keith's disappointment in his brother's way of life. He often appears rough and tough on the exterior when dealing with Gerard; nevertheless, deep down inside, Keith really does love his little brother, and just regrets what Gerard is doing. He knows that Gerard can be a better man than he has been.

Stephanie Glover-Mathis is a 40-year-old wife and mother. She is married to a successful businessman, Jason Mathis. The couple has two children: Troy, 15; and Allison, 9. Stephanie and Jason were high school sweethearts and continued their fairytale romance throughout college until eventually getting married. At first, Jason was a Prince Charming who just couldn't be anywhere else but beside his beautiful Stephanie. He adored her and often showed signs of his affection, which Stephanie appreciated. She felt special and loved by Jason.

Years prior, when the two were in college and had decided to get married, Stephanie had loyally supported Jason. She even declined the offer of an internship in another state because he did not want to move anywhere else at the time. Stephanie wanted to be married to Jason more than she wanted the internship. As a result, she remained at home and settled for her present set of circumstances.

As the years went by, Jason seemed to excel at pretty much anything that he put his mind to. He was never limited by any means; however, Stephanie realized that she had made some sacrifices to be with him. First of all, she had given up the internship. Then when the couple got married, Stephanie worked two jobs to support them when Jason was suddenly laid off from his job. For a while, she even put the brakes on her college career just to get them back on track financially. It is not being implied that Stephanie did not become successful. In fact, for a while she helped manage a very busy daycare with one of her friends and has some business and management skills under her belt. She is a competent and capable woman who just needed more support from her spouse.

Today Jason is co-owner of a thriving restaurant chain and is laying the foundation for other business ventures. Gradually through the years, Jason lost perspective and became less appreciative of the woman who helped him get as far as he has. He became successful and started to belittle his wife's dreams and goals, even telling Stephanie that she really didn't need to work anymore because he could practically do it all without her input anyway. This was the most upsetting to Stephanie, not because her husband said that she didn't have to work but because of him implying that she contributed little to what they had accomplished together or could accomplish in the long run. He made her feel worthless, and this was very painful.

In addition, Stephanie is not the slender, drop-dead gorgeous gal that she was over 20 years ago. She is still very attractive but has put on some weight. Her husband very seldom gets intimate with her and oftentimes falls asleep on the sofa while Stephanie is upstairs trying to figure out why her husband does not want her. She is drawing the conclusion that Jason does not love her anymore, or maybe not as much. Either way, the pain is almost unbearable. It feels demoralizing and embarrassing to not feel appreciated anymore by a man that used to call in the middle of the day just to say, "I love you."

The youngest of the Glovers is Robert. He is a 37-year-old lawyer who resides in California. Robbie is intelligent and driven. He owns a home near the beach and goes out at night just to sit on his patio and watch the sunset. He enjoys viewing landscapes. This is how Robbie clears his head from a hard day in the office. Sometimes he gets pretty lonely. Years earlier, Robbie broke up with his girlfriend because he felt that she was crowding his space. Now he wishes that he had someone special to share his life with, but he doesn't.

It is evident that the Glovers have their own individual set of problems and circumstances—some more or less than others. Overall, Mrs. Marguerite Glover loves all of her children dearly and tries to be supportive when times get rough. She knows that Keith is not as happy and confident as he used to be. She knows that Stephanie and Jason are not as close as they once were. It is evident more than the couple realizes. Mrs. Glover hopes that they will renew their bond and make things right between them.

Mrs. Glover longs for the day when her wayward son Gerard comes to his senses. She fears for his life everyday as he hustles and roams the streets. Most of the time she does not even know where he is. All she knows is that whatever he is up to only means trouble. From time to time, Gerard will stop by to see his mother and try to give her money. She always refuses, but he tries over and over to soften her up. This is one of those particular days...

"Mama, I got something for you." Gerard digs into his pocket.

"What are you up to, Gerard?" She inquires with a hint of suspicion.

"Can't I ever do anything that makes you happy, Mama? Why do you always think that I'm up to no good?"

"Whatever you bring into this house could not be good."

"Mama, I'm sorry you feel that way about your own son."

Keith is present and intervenes, "Gerard, put that money back into your pocket. Mama doesn't want that."

"Shouldn't you be at 'work' or something like that?" Gerard sarcastically utters.

"Don't start, man," Keith warns.

"Look at you—standing in a tollbooth all day," Gerard chuckles.

Keith defends, "At least I have a real job!"

Gerard fires back, "Real job? What's a real job? Busting my behind all day with nothing to show for it? No, Keith, that ain't work to me. I can go out there and make in one day what you don't even bring home in two weeks."

"Yeah, well, at least I don't have people looking for me because I owe them money. At least I don't have to always look over my shoulder because I'm doing something wrong."

"Oh yeah, I forgot how perfect you are! I may not have lived like you, but I'm a man just the same!" Gerard shouts.

"I don't think so, Gerard. You've spent your whole life hustling for every nickel and dime you could get, but you never tried to be productive with anything! Whatever requires a little bit of effort on your part makes you run in the opposite direction. You're a sorry and lazy excuse for a man!"

"And you are all washed up! Look what they did to you at that factory! For ten years, you nearly killed yourself for those people working all those long hours, and they still didn't keep you! You got kicked to the curb! Or should I be more politically correct and say you were 'downsized'?" Gerard insults.

"That's it! I have had it with you! I am ten times the man you'll ever be!" Keith expresses.

Their mother intervenes and holds Keith back. She tells him to calm down.

Keith tells his brother, "You are my brother, but I'm going to tell it like it is. There's nothing good coming your way, man—not at the rate you're going. You're on a collision course, and real soon you're gonna crash. I won't be around to pick up the pieces."

Keith gives his brother a stern look and then backs off. He turns away. Giving his mother a kiss on the cheek, Keith says, "I'll see you later, Mama. I love you. Bye."

Gerard watches his older brother leave as he cuts his eyes at Keith with disdain.

Mrs. Glover shakes her head and asks Gerard, "Why must you always do this to Keith?"

"Do what?" Gerard defends. "I didn't do anything to him."

"Oh, stop acting like you don't know what you've done! You like upsetting your brother, and now he has to go to work with your nonsense on his mind! He already has enough problems as it is."

"Mama, let me ask you a question. If I were more like Keith, would you love me more than you do now? Would I get all the hugs and kisses on the cheek like he does?" Gerard tests his mother's depth of feelings towards him.

She comes closer and points her finger in Gerard's face with her response. "Gerard, don't play with me, son. How dare you ask me such a question? I love you just the same as your brothers and sister. Whether you're worthy of it is another story, but I have always been the best mother you could ever have. So don't you dare belittle me and what I've done for you. I've tolerated your foolishness all this time, and a mother that didn't care at all would never have done that for you. I do love you, but just because I love you doesn't mean that I will continue to put up with this foolishness. Do you know how many nights I can't even sleep because I'm wondering what you're out there doing or if you're lying somewhere dead? You made a mess of your own life — not me or anybody else. So don't you come into my house taking me for some kind of fool and trying to make me feel like I owe you something else. I've done everything for you that I possibly could do."

Gerard cannot even look his mother in the eyes. He lowers his head and stares at the floor while she continues to scold him like a child.

"Don't you dare question my love or my loyalty. What you need to do is get yourself together. Learn to love yourself. For once, have some dignity about the way you carry yourself. You're a man—not a child."

Gerard is totally humiliated by his mother's speech. He does not speak another word but walks past her and goes out the door.

When her son leaves, Mrs. Glover starts to cry. She takes a look at her late husband's picture and shakes her head, mumbling to herself, "Charles would never stand for this." She walks down the hallway and sighs, "Oh Gerard, why do you break my heart like this?"

That Sunday evening, Mrs. Glover invites her family over for dinner. Keith and his family, Stephanie and her family, and Mrs. Glover's brother Earl never refuse her invitations. Mrs. Glover is quite a cook. During a mouth-watering feast, the family forgets about their problems and what is going on in their lives. They just enjoy each other's company.

Suddenly, the doorbell rings. Mrs. Glover answers the door and is alarmed to see a strange man. Keith can tell that his mother is surprised to see this visitor and rises up from his chair.

"Yes, how can I help you?" Mrs. Glover kindly inquires.

The man remains straight-faced and serious as he answers, "I'm looking for Gerard. Have you seen him today?"

Just then, Keith approaches and stands beside his mother. "What do you want with Gerard? He's not here."

The man replies, "Well, if and when you do see him, tell him that Jermaine was looking for him. I get the feeling that he's been dodging me… I wouldn't want to see anything happen to him."

Keith defends, "We don't need any threats, man. I suggest you get out of here. We haven't seen Gerard. Now go on. Get out of here."

The stranger slightly grins and mumbles, "Just remember what I said." He leaves the premises and leaves Mrs. Glover shaken up.

She asks Keith, "Do you think he'll really hurt him?"

Keith replies, "Mama, those kind of guys don't bite their tongues. If they say they're going to do something, they do it... I just hope Gerard doesn't end up in a body bag."

"Oh, Keith, why do you have to say that to me?"

"I'm sorry, Mama. It's the truth. Gerard puts himself in these kinds of situations. He asks for trouble."

"I don't want to hear anymore talk like this about Gerard, okay?"

Keith tries to pacify his mother by saying, "Mama, I know you love him, and it's hard for you to face this. The reality is that one day Gerard might not be here, and it's all because of what he does out there in those streets. I love him too but I just face the facts. You don't."

"I know as well as you do what could happen to him out there. I just can't bear to keep thinking about it... It hurts too much."

Keith places his arm around his mother and tells her, "I know it hurts, Mama. If I could I'd change things, but I can't. Gerard is not a little boy anymore for me to knock him upside his head when he steps out of line. He's a man, and only he can change himself."

At this point, Mrs. Glover is uneasy and tense, so she sits down at the table and tries to continue her meal. After a while, she gets up to clear the table. Keith's wife Cassandra offers to help her.

"Mama, I'll do it. You go relax."

"Oh, Cassandra, that's alright, honey. I'll do it. Thank you anyway."

As they drive home, Cassandra and Keith have a conversation about what happened.

"Keith, maybe we should've stayed a little while longer with your mother. She seemed so uneasy."

"I think that I upset her more than that guy did… I said some things that were true but that I probably should've kept to myself."

"Well, no mother wants to hear that her son could lose his life out there in the streets… It's a harsh reality."

"You know, baby, I just don't get it… My mother and father raised us the best they could and instilled good values in us. They taught us honesty and respect not just for everybody else, but for ourselves too. My brother is the complete opposite of everything that we were ever taught as children. I just don't understand him. He turned out all wrong. I've tried so much to reason with him, but he just won't listen to me. He won't even listen to Mama… When I think about it, she's real passive with him. I hardly ever see her put her foot down with him and let him have it."

"What if that was our situation—what would we do, Keith? Could we really cut off one of our children? Could we really abandon our son or our daughters if they really needed us to help them?"

"Cassandra, the whole family has tried to help Gerard, so it's not like we didn't care at all. He has never been abandoned by any of us. Mama always lets him come home to her when he's good and ready. She has never turned him away. Half the time she doesn't even know where that boy is. When he does show up, he'll stay a night or two and then leave again. We all love him, but frankly, I'm tired of him jerking this whole family around like he's been doing. As far as I'm concerned, I don't want anything to do with him until he shapes up. I've had enough now. It's one thing for him to mess up his own life and put himself in danger, but now he has this street trash coming to my mama's house. This has to stop right now."

The next day, Gerard is walking down the block when Jermaine approaches him. He is somewhat startled but remains calm. Jermaine pokes him in the shoulder as an insult and asks, "You got the money?"

"Here's half of it, man. I'll get you the rest later."

"I want it all now, Gerard!"

"Look, I don't have it, man! Just give me a few days, alright?"

Jermaine is not pleased. As a result, he turns and looks behind him. At the snap of a finger, two men get out of a Cadillac and approach Gerard.

Gerard nervously inquires, "Who are they? What's going on?"

Eventually, Gerard makes it to his sister's neighborhood and stumbles onto her doorstep.

Her son Troy looks out the window and tells his mother that Gerard is outside.

"I think he's hurt, Mom."

Stephanie immediately rises up and opens the door. She sighs, "Oh, Gerard. What happened to you? Get in here. Come on, Troy, help me get him in the house."

Stephanie had never seen her brother in such bad shape. She had always known him to act like a tough guy. This is the first time that she has ever seen Gerard in a vulnerable position. She leaves a note for her husband Jason to let him know that she has taken Gerard to the hospital.

"I don't wanna go to no hospital!" Gerard stubbornly objects.

"You can't even stand up, Gerard. You're going to get checked out by a doctor. My goodness, when Mama sees you, she's going to faint. She's just going to faint, I know it."

"I'm not sitting in some emergency room for five hours just so that some stupid doctor can patch me up with a band aid and send me home."

"You know, you are really working my last nerve here. You dragged yourself to my doorstep, barely able to stand up straight, and you don't think you need to see a doctor. You're the most stubborn person I've ever known, Gerard. I think you probably need more than a little band aid in your condition."

At the hospital, Stephanie and Troy sit with Gerard as they wait for the nurse to see them. Her daughter Allison is with a babysitter. Just then, Stephanie gets up.

"Troy, I'm going to go and call your dad okay? Just sit with your uncle, and I'll be right back."

Stephanie calls home, but there is no answer. She calls her husband's office, and he is still there.

"Hello?" Jason answers.

"It's me. I just called home, but you weren't there so I knew you'd have to be at the office… I left a note that you can disregard now."

"Where are you?"

"I'm at the hospital with Gerard."

"What happened?"

"Let's just say that he didn't exactly have a great day."

"Oh, please don't even tell me. I can already figure it out… He must be pretty banged up, huh?" Jason assumes.

"Yeah, he is. He showed up on our doorstep. He said he got kicked in the ribs."

"That brother of yours is something else. I don't even know why you deal with him."

"Jason, what was I supposed to do, leave him on our doorstep? I gotta go. Mama's here."

Mrs. Glover forgets about how rotten and horrible everyone thinks her son is and lovingly assists him. "Gerard, look at you! Oh, this is terrible!"

"Mama, please stop. You're making me feel worse than I already do… I just got a busted lip."

Troy intervenes, "Grandma, Uncle Gerard is really hurt—more than he's telling you."

"I know he is. He's just trying to be tough."

The nurse on duty cleans up Gerard's lip as they await the doctor's evaluation.

"Well, you're very fortunate. There are no fractures or broken ribs. However, I would suggest that you take it easy for a few days and not do too much. I'm going to prescribe something for the pain. Then you're free to go."

For a few days, Gerard decides to lay low. He sleeps all day and only gets up to eat. Mrs. Glover assists him as if he were a helpless baby.

"You know, you could've been dead? That man could've killed you... You better be glad that he didn't decide to do you in, Gerard. Stay out of trouble!"

"I ain't gonna let him scare me, Mama. I ain't no punk. Besides, once I pay him what I owe I'll be done with him anyway."

"Would you think about what you just said? You just got the living daylights beaten out of you. You shouldn't be out there in those streets anyway. What you need to do is find a real job—"

"You sound just like Mr. Perfect. Keith is always talking about that 'real job' stuff. I don't wanna hear it. I have my own way of survival. He has his. Each man for himself."

"Gerard, I pity you, son. I truly do... You be here when I get back."

"Where are you going?"

"To the store. I forgot that you eat like a horse. I'm going to get some groceries."

"Hey, Mama, bring me back some chocolate chip cookies. No—make that Oreos. That's what I want, some Oreo cookies."

Mrs. Glover ignores her son's request and walks out the door. As she unlocks her car door, Mr. Sanders greets her. He is walking his dog down the block.

"Hello, Marguerite."

"Hi, Bartholomew."

The dog barks as Mrs. Glover reaches down to pet him. "Oh, what a cutie. I didn't know that you had a dog."

"I didn't have one until a few weeks ago. My granddaughter gave him to me. Her dog had some puppies. I figured that it would be nice to have someone else in the house other than me. I like the sound of him in the mornings. He wakes me up."

"Oh, I'll bet he does," Mrs. Glover replies. After the small talk, Mr. Sanders moves on.

"Take care, Marguerite."

"You do the same, Bartholomew."

Mr. Bartholomew Sanders is a widower. His wife Betsy died five years earlier of lung cancer. They have three adult children: Marvin, Angela and Carlton. He has seven grandchildren. Mr. Sanders lives alone, with the exception of his new dog. He is a retired electrical engineer. His deceased wife was a medical secretary. Mr. Sanders keeps himself strong and positive by pre-occupying his time with hobbies such as fishing, playing chess with his friend Thomas Grady, cooking and, of course, taking his new dog Max for his daily walk.

When Mrs. Glover returns from the supermarket, Gerard is up and about. He is still sore from the beating but manages to make his way to the sofa to watch TV. He opens the door for his mother and takes two of the bags from her hand. She places the third bag on the countertop and informs him, "Gerard, they're hiring at the store."

"What?" he questions as if he didn't hear Mrs. Glover.

"Newman's is hiring. There's a big sign in the window. They're hiring for the produce section and the night crew."

"That don't interest me." Gerard arrogantly proclaims.

Mrs. Glover angrily replies, "Well, excuse me, but the last time I checked you hadn't become rich overnight!"

"Mama, I can make more money out there on those streets than at some supermarket washing fruit and mopping floors with some fake smile on my face."

"If your father could only see what you've become... No one misses your father as much as I do, but I must say that I'm glad that he doesn't have to see you like this. It would break his heart. It's certainly broken mine."

Mrs. Glover lowers her head in despair and goes into the kitchen to start dinner. Gerard observes his mother's countenance for a while. She does not speak to him. He feels guilty about what he said. He rises up from the sofa and enters the kitchen. Gerard places his arm around his mother and tells her, "I'll go check it out."

"Check what out? The job?"

"Yeah, I'll go to Newman's in the morning."

Later that night, Gerard thinks that his mother is in her room sleeping. She is awake and can overhear his conversation with someone on the phone.

"I know man, my Mama told me about working at Newman's. You know, that supermarket across town?"

"They don't pay good money, man," informs the anonymous person. "I could really set you up with something. You in?"

Gerard is tempted but replies, "I don't know. I'll let you know, okay?"

"You're getting soft."

"No, no it's nothing like that. Me soft? Are you out of your mind? I'm doing this for her—my mother. She wants me to find a 'real' job and turn into Mr. Perfect like that brother of mine. Anyway, I'll get back with you on that. Later."

True enough, that next morning Gerard gets up early and heads down to Newman's Supermarket to fill out an application. When he arrives, he is tempted to walk out the door before even speaking with the manager. Then he thinks of his mother and how disappointed she would be if he gave up.

Gerard approaches the manager, "Good morning. I'd like an application, please."

Mr. Douglas gives Gerard an application and inquires, "What kind of experience do you have? Can you cashier or stock shelves for me?"

Gerard feels humiliated by such a question. It hurts his pride to reply, "Yeah, I can do those things." They seem so simple to him.

Mr. Douglas directs Gerard to the table to fill out the application. "When you're done, bring it back over to me so that I can look at it."

Gerard spends 15 minutes completing the application. The hardest question is about his criminal background. He wants to circle 'no' but does not feel right lying about his past. Gerard does the right thing and honestly replies 'yes' to the question and then gives a brief explanation of his offense. When he turns in the application, he is convinced that Mr. Douglas will take one look at this and turn him away. To his surprise, Gerard is offered a position.

"Can you work some nights or evenings?" Mr. Douglas asks, "I've pretty much filled up most of the day shifts. I'll hire you if you can pull a couple of nights for me."

Gerard accepts and starts the next day on the evening shift as a crewmember. He has his doubts but forces himself to do this because of his mother.

For a few weeks, everything goes well. Gerard looks at his first paycheck and sighs. "Man, it took me two weeks to draw a $550 paycheck. I gotta get used to this." Gerard is used to his quick money schemes and has to adjust to actually working hard for a living.

Keith has been observing his brother's behavior and is too proud to admit that he is impressed by Gerard's transformation—even if Gerard did not do it on his own initiative. Their mother coaxed him into the job, and so far he is complying with her wishes to stay on a straight path. She just wants her son to do better than hanging out on the street corners getting into trouble or wasting time being unproductive.

That same day Gerard offers his mother part of his paycheck, but she refuses. "No, you keep that and open up a bank account or something."

"Mama, you gotta take something from me. Here, at least take $100 for some groceries."

"No, Gerard, you keep that money and use it wisely… Do you know how proud I am of you, son? This is the first time in years that I could actually say this to you. You've proven everybody wrong."

"I'm sure I did. I know everybody's watching me like a hawk."

That evening, Mr. Sanders from down the block knocks on Mrs. Glover's door. He seems a bit worried.

"Hello, Bartholomew, how are you?"

"Well, unfortunately, I'm a bit worried about Max. I can't find him."

"Your dog Max is gone?"

"Yes, I guess that I must've left the backdoor slightly opened without realizing it. That's the only way for him to have gotten out. Anyway, I came by to ask if you could be on the lookout for me. I've already put up some flyers. Hopefully, he'll wander back home somehow. I feel so bad for him. He's just a puppy."

Mr. Sanders stays for a cup of coffee. After knowing Mrs. Glover for five years and just simply passing by and waving, he realizes that they have a lot in common. They actually sit there and talk about how much it hurts to feel lonely. This is their first real conversation.

"Betsy was my best friend in this whole world. She was some kind of woman. When she died, I just knew that my life was over. I knew that I would never be the same man without her. I loved my wife more than anything in this world. I'd give anything just to have her back. She always did little things to let me know that she still cared about me just as much as the day we met. Betsy never took me for granted."

"It's hard to lose someone that you've spent your whole life with isn't it?" Mrs. Glover reiterates. "Charles and I would just sit for hours and talk about anything. We used to walk in the park and hold hands like two teenagers in love... It's hard not to do those things anymore. I truly miss him. Words just cannot express what I've been going through. If I didn't have my children, I don't know what I'd do. They tell me that I keep them going, but if they only knew just what they do for me, too."

After an hour or so, Mr. Sanders takes his leave.

He did eventually recover his dog Max. A neighbor found Max and returned him to Mr. Sanders.

Occasionally, he finds himself showing up at Mrs. Glover's doorstep just to talk. He reasons with himself that he has made a new friend, and it actually feels good to have someone to confide in.

One Sunday evening, as usual, Mrs. Glover invites her family to dinner. This particular day, Mr. Sanders is one of her guests as well. When he arrives, Keith shows a bit of surprise by raising his eyebrow. He glances over at his wife Cassandra and slightly, discreetly, nods his head towards Mr. Sanders as if to communicate, 'What is he doing here?'

Cassandra knows exactly what Keith is implying and just grins at him. She shakes her head and whispers, "Be nice."

Mrs. Glover anxiously welcomes her guest. As Mr. Sanders says hello, the family members extend their hospitality. Keith is somewhat suspicious even though he knows Mr. Sanders. He has never seen him at his mother's home before. Gerard is too preoccupied with the thought of that juicy meatloaf and gravy going into his stomach that he could care less why their neighbor is at his mother's house. He is more than ready to eat dinner while everyone else scopes out Mr. Sanders, looking as handsome as could be. The man even brings a dessert.

"Marguerite, I love to bake, so I hope you like this. It's Betsy's recipe—peach cobbler."

"Oh, thank you. That was very thoughtful of you, Bartholomew. Please, have a seat. We're just about ready to get started with dinner."

Throughout the course of the meal, Mr. Sanders relates life experiences with the family and tries to create a warm atmosphere among them. He cannot deny the fact that his mind has been on Mrs. Glover lately. He feels somewhat guilty because it is confusing for him to grieve over a beloved wife and to feel butterflies for a neighbor who used to just be someone to say hello to.

Stephanie actually likes Mr. Sanders and engages in a deep conversation with him about social issues. They swap opinions and laughter for a large portion of the evening. Keith remains more quiet than usual, and it is noticed by his wife and mother.

Gerard manages to gulp down two helpings of Mr. Sanders's peach cobbler after having two full plates of food. He commends, "Mr. Sanders, I have to give it you—this is pretty good. You have a talent here."

"Oh, I wouldn't go that far as to say it's a talent. My late wife was the real cook. I just improvise these days without her." There is complete silence. Suddenly, Mr. Sanders politely tells the family, "Well, I'd best be on my way now. I have thoroughly enjoyed spending this wonderful evening with you all. Thank you, Marguerite. Dinner was absolutely delicious."

Mr. Sanders and Mrs. Glover share a brief moment in La-La Land. Everyone can see that Mr. Sanders and their mother like each other. Keith observes a glow in her eyes that he hasn't seen since his father was alive.

"Please, don't be a stranger, Bartholomew. Come again."

"Thank you, Marguerite. I appreciate your hospitality. You're a wonderful person."

Mr. Sanders leaves as Mrs. Glover watches him walk down the sidewalk. He only lives a few blocks down.

One night, Robbie Glover calls from California and Gerard answers the phone. It must be acknowledged that the two men have had their share of squabbles. Gerard views Robbie as a pompous snob who forgot where he came from. Robbie describes Gerard as a work NOT in progress. Gerard can remember something that his younger brother said to him the last time they spoke. Robbie expressed, "Where do you get off telling me that I forgot where I came from? I'm pretty secure with myself, and I know exactly who I am. You're just mad because you wouldn't allow your own life to turn out half as good as mine. When I was a little kid, I used to look up to you man. Now I feel sorry for you because you fail to see what you've become. You're pitiful."

"Hello?" Gerard answers the phone.

Immediately Robbie knows that it is his brother. He hesitates to speak but then responds, "Gerard, is Mama there?"

"Oh, I can't even get a hello from you now... I see how you are, man."

"Gerard, please, not now, okay?"

"Mama is not here. She went shopping with one of her friends. I'll tell her you called."

"Please do." Robbie hangs up the phone. He is calling to tell his mother that he wants to come home and spend a week with the family. Robbie comes home to everyone's pleasure—except for Gerard. He could really care less. Robbie and Keith have always maintained a close relationship and get to spend quality time together. Deep within, Gerard observes and envies the bond between his two brothers and feels bitter that they think so little of him.

Meanwhile, Stephanie and her husband Jason attend a banquet in honor of Michael Miller, one of Jason's colleagues. This particular colleague is also helping Jason to launch a new business. Stephanie is not very fond of Michael for several reasons. One reason is the way that he treats his wife, Susan. Oftentimes, he leaves her at home with their children while he takes vacations here and there with fellow colleagues and cronies. When Susan does accompany her husband anywhere, Michael belittles her and strips her of every shred of dignity. Susan Miller is probably not as shy as she pretends to be in the presence of her husband and his friends. Stephanie assumes that this is a façade that Susan presents to the public. It is an image of an overly submissive wife who does not stand beside her husband as a complement but rather behind him as a shadow.

Granted, things have not been great and wonderful between Stephanie and Jason either; nevertheless, Jason does not play the role of a tyrant. He has not been very loving, supportive or affectionate lately, but has never been domineering towards Stephanie. Actually, his disposition is more passive and indifferent — a little too indifferent. Stephanie feels lonely and longs for her hus-

29

band to be romantic again. Time has molded him into a money-hungry, ambitious man who finds more pleasure in business than family. He takes everyone for granted, especially Stephanie. He is used to her undying loyalty and expects it at this point. He has never seen it any other way.

Driving home from the banquet, Stephanie makes a proposal to her husband. "Honey, why don't we go away for a while—just the two of us?"

"Sweetheart, you know that I have the Grant deal coming up soon. That man has money to burn, and I want some of it. I can't concentrate on that and a vacation right now."

Stephanie cannot believe how her husband is speaking. She changes the subject and reminisces on a more humble beginning for the two of them. "Jason, do you remember how things were for us when we first got married?"

"I try not to remember it," he admits.

"We had that nice little apartment a few blocks from the campus... I think about how much we really had, although it seemed as if we had very little."

"Stephanie, I brought you out of that life, didn't I? What matters is now."

Stephanie politely reminds her husband, "We worked together, and you know that."

"What are you being so uptight about?"

"You just said that YOU brought me out of that life," Stephanie clarifies.

"Okay, and your point is what?" Jason questions.

"Have you forgotten that I worked two jobs when you lost yours? I did it willingly, and I'd do it again if I had to."

"Well, then what are you complaining about, Stephanie?" Jason is becoming irritated.

"You seem to forget that before you started kissing up to big corporate executives, we had a pretty humble life — just the two of us. We scraped for every penny that we could get and gladly accepted whatever our parents could give us. Jason, you're not the same man that I knew back then. Back then you knew the value of a dollar and could actually hold onto one. Remember when you had to match up one or two pairs of pants with every single jacket in your closet with no complaints?"

"For heaven's sake, Stephanie, would you just stop it? You make it seem as if I'm this horrible person."

"I didn't say that. You're just not the same person."

"Maybe I'm not! What's so wrong with that? You can stay in the past if you want to, but I choose a different route… I made sure that I wasn't going to struggle like our folks did."

"Jason, there is nothing wrong with being successful. What's wrong is when a person forgets who he is and what he stands for, or used to stand for."

"If you're so unhappy with what I've become, then why don't you just call it quits?"

Stephanie is shocked. "What?"

"If you don't like what kind of man I've become, then divorce me."

"Jason, I love you. I don't want a divorce."

"Then stop hassling me! How could you be so ungrateful for what we have?"

"I'm not ungrateful, Jason. I just want my husband back!"

"I'm right here in front of you!"

"No, I live with a complete stranger! When is the last time that we have actually been intimate with each other? You've forgotten how to be romantic altogether!"

"Nonsense! Just two weeks ago, I brought home a pearl necklace for you and some matching earrings. Oh, and what about the anniversary gift?"

"Jason, you handed me the box and went upstairs to go watch TV. You did it because it was safe."

"Safe?"

"You've always gotten me anniversary gifts, year after year. In the past, you did it because you actually wanted to. Now you do it because you feel that you have to so that I won't complain. There's a big difference, and don't think for one minute that I don't see it."

"What do you want from me, Stephanie?"

She sarcastically replies, "Well, if it's not too much, I'd actually like for you to wake up one morning and be holding me in your arms. I'd like for you to touch me like it's the last thing you'll ever get to do. I want you to want me again, Jason. For once, I want you to forget that you're a successful businessman with tons of colleagues and business accounts. I want you to remember that you married a girl named Stephanie Glover and promised to take care of her the rest of her life…You've given me every material thing that I could possibly own. I just want you, Jason. If I have to live in a cardboard shack and eat wish sandwiches, I'll do it with you. That's how we started, anyway. Remember? I just want you back."

Briefly, Jason looks away as his wife reveals what she wants from him at this point in their marriage. He turns and looks into her eyes. "Stephanie, I do care about you, but it's just not the same... It's just not the same."

She boldly asks, "Is there someone else?"

Jason shakes his head, "No, there's no one else... For a long time now, I've felt this way. I just couldn't tell you."

"I guess it's hard to tell somebody that you just don't love them anymore. Is that what you want to tell me?"

"I never said that I didn't love you."

"But you're not in love with me, right?"

Jason hesitates to answer.

Stephanie continues, "Listen, I know that I'm not exactly a size six anymore, Jason. My body has changed, yes, but I haven't. Do you think that I don't notice the little spare tire that you're getting in the midsection? You stayed skinny, slim and trim for so long, and now you're finally putting on a little weight. You know how I feel about that? I just see my husband aging. That's all I see, but it doesn't change my feelings by any means. You're still the love of my life, Jason—whether you have washboard abs or love handles. I still love you just as the day I married you... I'm not going to apologize for having larger hips or a fuller figure. I don't have to look like Miss Universe at this point in my life in order to feel okay with myself. I like who I am regardless of my size. Maybe that's what you need to do—like me again. Maybe you'll actually see something special on the inside instead of on the outside."

Jason and Stephanie separate. They have some issues between them that they are not resolving properly; therefore, the couple spends some time apart. Jason temporarily moves in with a single buddy. Stephanie is heartbroken; nevertheless, she must stay strong not only for herself but for the sake of the children. Jason is too proud to admit that he has done a lot of things wrong. He is afraid that his wife can see a side of him that he denies. Jason does not want to view himself as a shallow person. It is the hardest thing to do. After all, we never see ourselves the way other people do.

Stephanie pours out her heart to her mother. Mrs. Glover shows compassion towards her daughter.

"Stephanie, I want you to be happy whether Jason is around or not. I know that you love him, and you should, because he's your husband and the father of your children, but just remember that he doesn't make you who you are. It's up to you to be content with yourself."

"He's just changed so much, and it was so gradual… I really can't pinpoint a particular time frame for this. It just happened. For years, I watched my marriage grow distant. I watched my husband forget how to love me. I just accepted it all and became a passive, silent partner… Mama, I want to call him so bad. I'm even trying to be angry with him for leaving, but I love him so much. I just want to hold him in my arms and not let go. I'm trying to be strong, but it's so hard."

"I know, baby, I know. You're hurting now, but in the long run you will come out of this stronger, regardless of Jason returning or not."

"If I approach him and he refuses to come home, then I'd feel like such a fool, Mama. What if he never comes back? I just can't bear the thought of knowing that he wouldn't."

"Remember what I said—Jason doesn't make you who you are. For years now you've sat on the sidelines and tolerated this treatment from him because you thought you had to. Let me tell you something, baby: loyalty does not mean surrender. In other words, it's perfectly fine to be loyal to someone you love, but no one should expect you to deny yourself happiness just for their sake. You don't have to give up your own dreams or desires for the sake of someone else. You can be loyal, but don't surrender or give up on yourself. How would you benefit from giving the world to someone else when you haven't done a single thing for yourself? You've made every sacrifice possible for your husband, and this is the thanks you get for all of that—him leaving you. If Jason wants to come back and patch things up, then that's wonderful. If he doesn't come back, then you find the resolve to move on without him. It can be done."

Months pass, and the Glover family seem to be thriving as much as possible. One day, Mrs. Glover is taking groceries in from her car when Mr. Sanders greets her.

"Hello, Marguerite, how are you today?"

She politely responds but deliberately keeps things brief between them. She had expected him to come around more often since he seemed to enjoy her company. It has been over two months since she had Mr. Sanders over for dinner. He has not talked to her since that time.

"Marguerite, let me help you with those bags."

"No, it's okay. I can do it myself, Bartholomew."

He senses some agitation from Mrs. Glover and backs away. He stands there not knowing what else to do. Finally, Mr. Sanders expresses himself.

"Marguerite, can we go inside and talk? It's really important."

She invites him in and makes a pot of coffee.

"So, what is it that's so important, Bartholomew?"

"Well, lately I've been doing a lot of thinking, and I've drawn the conclusion that I haven't been totally honest with myself or with you. You see, that night when we sat and talked, it seemed as if I had been revitalized. I felt as if I could breathe again. I wasn't a sad, lonely, old man anymore. I had found a friend, someone that I could just sit and talk to. I haven't had that since my wife died. I have buddies, but it's just not the same as spending time with you. I got scared, especially after you had me over for dinner with your family. At that point, I thought of you more often than before. That scared me, Marguerite. I never expected to feel attracted to anyone at this point in my life… I guess what I'm stumbling over here is the fact that I really like you and would like to get to know you much better…if you'd like to get to know me better."

"Actually, I noticed that you hadn't been around in a while. I was somewhat disappointed."

"Well, I deliberately did that because I was afraid of what I was feeling. I guess I didn't know how to face you, Marguerite. I'm sorry… I hope that what I've said makes some kind of sense to you."

"It does," Mrs. Glover replies. She doesn't say another word, and Mr. Sanders is embarrassed that he has opened up his heart like this.

"Good day, Marguerite." He turns and walks away since Mrs. Glover is remaining silent. He assumes that she is not interested in him.

"So will you be joining us this Sunday?" she inquires.

Mr. Sanders turns back around with a coy grin on his face and replies, "I sure will."

Mrs. Glover generously offers, "I'll prepare one of your favorite meals. What do you like?"

"Fried chicken," Mr. Sanders answers.

As he continues down the block, Mrs. Glover giggles to herself and goes into the house. She mumbles, "Why am I not surprised? Every man that I know loves fried chicken."

That Sunday, Mr. Sanders joins the family once again for dinner. Mrs. Glover has prepared a wonderful, scrumptious meal: fried chicken, mashed potatoes and gravy, collard greens, cornbread, potato salad, and a nice chocolate cake for dessert.

Keith seems to be having some trouble with his mother's new relationship. He does not try to open up to Mr. Sanders. This is noticeable, so Mr. Sanders attempts to have a conversation with Keith. It does not go well and is very short-lived. To break the tension, Keith's wife Cassandra starts a new subject. Mrs. Glover picks up on her daughter-in-law's attempt and plays along. Once again, the conversation has switched gears.

Gerard rises up from the table and excuses himself. "I have to go to work, so I'll have to cut this short. Mama, that was excellent, just excellent. Make sure that you save me some of that chicken for later when I get home."

"I always save the food for you. You're the skinniest person in here, with the biggest appetite." Mrs. Glover teases.

Mr. Sanders smirks. He admires Mrs. Glover's sense of humor. When he is about to leave, he tells Mrs. Glover, "I had a wonderful time once again. Marguerite, you're the best. Thank you."

"Oh, anytime. You're always welcome."

"Goodnight, dear." Mr. Sanders uses this term of endearment towards Mrs. Glover to Keith's dislike.

Keith shakes his head and mocks Mr. Sanders. He whispers to his wife, "He called her 'dear.'"

Cassandra grumbles, "I guess we better lock him up for doing that, huh?" She is being sarcastic. "Honey, will you please relax? Your mother hasn't been this happy in years."

"Well, I don't like it."

"But she does." Cassandra adds, "Leave her alone."

After Mr. Sanders leaves, Mrs. Glover is quiet for a moment. Then she speaks to her son, "You know, you could've been a little bit nicer to Bartholomew. He tried real hard to open up to you. For years, you've always been very pleasant with him. Why now all of a sudden do you treat him with indifference? What has he done so wrong, Keith?"

"I just don't like what I'm seeing."

"What you are seeing is a nice man dropping by for Sunday dinner. That is all you see because that's all it is."

"Mama, don't you stand there and tell me that Mr. Sanders only likes your fried chicken. He likes more than that. He comes around to get a dose of good ol' Marguerite."

"Keith, stop it!" Mrs. Glover angrily commands. "You have no right to speak of him that way! I won't have it!"

Cassandra starts to clear the table. She goes into the kitchen so that Keith and his mother can discuss this further.

"I'm sorry, it's just that I worry about you."

"Why?"

"Mama, Daddy's been gone for a while now, and I know that you're lonely. I don't want you to fall for some man and get yourself all emotionally charged up like that. He can't replace Daddy. You know that."

Mrs. Glover sets the record straight. "Keith, let me tell you something. First of all, I can't replace Charles with any man, and I'm certainly not trying to. The second thing is this: I've been a grown woman for quite a long time now, and I'm pretty capable of taking care of myself and my own emotions. I'm not naïve and ignorant. I like Bartholomew's company, and that's no crime."

"I just don't want you to get hurt, Mama."

"Why do I have to? Unless you know something about him that I don't, it's safe to say that Bartholomew is a very decent man. I like him, and he likes me. What makes you think that's so bad?"

"I don't know, Mama, I just didn't think that at this point in your life you'd be doing this kind of stuff."

"Doing what? Living? I'm a 68-year-old woman who still appreciates what time I have left. I haven't croaked yet! You should be ashamed of yourself, Keith. It's like you're telling your mother not to be happy anymore just because she's old."

"That's not what I'm saying. You're taking the whole thing out of context."

"And you're being unreasonable! Can you sit here and tell me that if you passed away, you wouldn't want Cassandra to be happy again with somebody if that person happened to come along? Would you honestly want your wife to spend the rest of her life without a companion?" Cassandra peeps around from the kitchen and awaits an answer from her husband.

Keith giggles and replies, "Oh no, you're not going to put her in this. That's a totally different situation."

"What makes it so different, Keith?" Mrs. Glover probes.

"She's my wife. You're my mother. You spent your life with my father, and it's just not easy to see you with some other man. It's just hard, Mama. No one can measure up to my Daddy, and no one else is good enough for you."

"You let me be the judge of that."

"I love you, and I just don't think he's good enough."

"If I had any reservations about Bartholomew Sanders, he wouldn't have set foot into this house from the very start. Do you understand me? Am I making myself clear, Keith?"

Keith is very disturbed. His wife is surprised to see him acting this way. She knew that he had reservations about Mr. Sanders and his mother courting, but Cassandra did not realize how deep these feelings were. Keith misses his father and is afraid that his mother's sense of loyalty to her late husband will be diminished by her newfound relationship. Mrs. Glover sympathizes with her son and takes him into her arms. She embraces him like a little child needing comfort from his mother.

"Keith, I understand your feelings and take them into consideration, but I feel that you're overreacting to this whole thing. I know that you miss your father very much. I miss him, too.

Believe me, I do. He was my husband and my best friend in this whole world. He's irreplaceable, baby. Bartholomew is not a replacement. He's a kind, gentle man who enjoys my company. Can't you understand that?"

"I guess I just need more time to get used to him being around you so much. I feel that my father's place has been taken."

"Bartholomew and I have a great understanding. He's not trying to be your father. He's just a nice man who likes spending time with your mother. Please be kinder. I'm asking you to please be kinder to him—at least for my sake."

One evening, Mr. Sanders is mowing the lawn for Mrs. Glover. He is full of vigor and energy. Keith usually does this job for his mother. As he enters the house, he greets his mother and gives her a kiss on the cheek. "Hey Mama, this kitchen smells so good."

"You're welcome to join us. Pull up a chair. Dinner will be ready real soon."

"No, I'm just going to wait until I go home since Cassandra is probably cooking something anyway."

"Oh, alright. Take some food with you. Save her some time. After all, she works too. I'm sure she's tired... Keith, do you remember that girl Bernice Spencer?"

Keith's mind is somewhere else. He is sitting in a recliner watching Mr. Sanders mow the lawn. He has a clear view of him as he peers out the window. Mrs. Glover rambles on about one of Keith's former girlfriends, before he met Cassandra. He is not even listening to her although he pretends to be.

"Keith, I dyed my hair red."

"Uhh-huh…what?"

"I just said that to see how you'd react since you haven't been listening to a thing that I said all this time. I saw Bernice Spencer today at the beauty parlor. She's doing well."

"Bernice Spencer?"

"Bernice Spencer-Hayden. She's married to a doctor."

"Good for her. I haven't seen her in a long, long time."

"She asked about you and said that she'd like for you and Cassandra to have dinner sometime with her and her husband. She gave me her number."

Keith has drifted again. His mother inquires, "What's wrong with you today? You seem so distracted."

"Mama, I came over here to do the lawn. That's why I'm here. Did you forget?"

"Well, Bartholomew offered to do it. I'm sorry, I didn't think it was a big deal."

"I always do the lawn for you. It's never been an issue."

Mrs. Glover realizes that her son is a bit jealous of Mr. Sanders. She tells him, "Keith, he offered to do it. I think that was nice of him."

"That old man is going to break his back out there."

"Well, he looks fine to me. So far, he's already done the backyard."

"No, no way."

"What is wrong with you? Why would I lie? Go back there and look at it. It looks real good—just like you would do."

Keith goes outside to the backyard and evaluates the quality of Mr. Sanders's work. He must admit that Mr. Sanders didn't miss a patch of grass. The lawn is smooth and leveled.

Keith stays a little bit longer so that his mother can give him food to take home for dinner. This is just about the time when Mr. Sanders finishes the lawn. He comes into the front door and wipes his forehead with a rag. He is sweating.

"Here, I poured you a nice, cool glass of tea."

"Thank you, Marguerite."

Mr. Sanders says hello to Keith as he nods his head to Mr. Sanders without speaking. "I'm going to leave now, Mama. Goodbye, Mr. Sanders."

"Excuse me, may I have a word with you, Keith? Do you mind?"

Keith looks at his mother as he wonders what Mr. Sanders has to say. She offers to leave the room.

"No, Mama, that's okay. We can go outside and talk since I'm on my way out. Let's go outside, Mr. Sanders."

As they stand outside on the front porch, Mr. Sanders speaks. "Keith, I don't beat around the bush, so I'll just say exactly what's on my mind. I've been sensing some ill feelings between us. It seems as if you aren't particularly fond of me these days. I remember always having a pleasant experience with you. I never knew you really well, but you were always cordial towards me in the past… Are you uncomfortable with me dating your mother?"

Keith hesitates at first but admits, "Well, I'm not exactly thrilled about it. I just didn't expect it, I guess. The only man I could ever see her with was my father, and he's not here. I wish he were here. She misses him, and so do I. We were very close."

"I know it must be hard on you. When my kids lost their mother, it was hard on them too. We were a very close family."

"If you don't mind me asking, how do they feel about this whole thing with you and my mother?"

"Truthfully, they're happy for me. Yes, they miss their mother, but they realize that I will never forget her or stop loving her. There will always be a special place in my heart for her. They know that. They have no reservations towards Marguerite. In fact, they've even met your mother."

"Really?"

"Yes, last week. My daughter Angela had us over for dinner. It was quite an evening. They got along so well with your mother... I would like to have that kind of rapport with you too. You seem to be the only one who is not particularly fond of this situation. I hope that you will change your mind and give me a chance."

Keith feels like crawling under a rock. He is so embarrassed by his behavior and apologizes to Mr. Sanders without hesitation.

"Keith, it's alright. I accept your apology. Hey, you're only human. I respect your feelings, but let me reassure you that your mother is not dealing with a bad guy here."

Keith manages to smile at Mr. Sanders and shakes his hand. He feels better about the situation. "I hear that you like fishing?"

"Oh yes, it's a hobby of mine. Your mother must've told you, huh?"

Keith replies, "Yes, she did. Why don't we go this weekend—just you and me? We can get to know each other better."

Mr. Sanders and Keith go fishing that Saturday morning and get to learn about each other. Keith even expresses his feelings about losing his job recently and having to be downsized.

"For ten years I proved myself at that place, and then they just let me go. I got replaced by machines. Since when did computers and machines take the place of good ol' common sense and ingenuity?"

"Well, it can be hard to understand a situation like that, but you must keep a positive outlook on things. You do have a job to go to everyday, even if it's not what you really want. At least you have a loving, supportive wife who is willing to work side by side with you. You have three wonderful kids who adore you, and your mother absolutely takes pride in you. She is so proud of you… You have a lot to be thankful for, Keith. Remember that. It's okay to do what you're doing as long as you make a living. That's your objective, right, to put food on your table?"

"Yes, sir."

"Well, then, continue and learn how to enjoy what you do until you can do better. It's not as bad as it seems."

Keith thinks about what he has been told and nods in agreement. "You're right. You're absolutely right."

Gerard is about to leave work after collecting his paycheck from his supervisor. One of his co-workers, Teresa Valdez, approaches him. "Hey, what's going on?"

"Nothing much, just collecting my paycheck. What time do you get off?"

Teresa answers, "In two hours. I work until seven tonight."

Gerard and Teresa become friends. Even though he is tempted sometimes to quit the job, he keeps in mind how disappointed his mother would be if he did so. Also, he likes Teresa and figures that being around her at work is a good way to spend time with her.

"Teresa, do you have any plans tonight?"

"Other than curling up on my sofa and watching TV, no, I have no plans."

"Well, you ain't sitting in front of a TV set tonight. I'm taking you to see a movie. I'll take you out to dinner too."

Teresa flashes her bright smile and shows pearly white teeth. She is a beautiful Hispanic woman in her early thirties. She has two children, a 12-year-old son and a 5-year-old daughter. Gerard does not know this.

"I can't go anywhere. I have to be with my kids."

49

"Oh, well, let's take them too."

Teresa cannot believe what she is hearing. "Wow, you're the first to say that. Guys don't usually agree to my kids tagging along on a date. Well, this is not a date, right? We're just going on a friendly outing, right?"

Gerard replies, "Something like that."

When Teresa gets home, her mother is there with the children. She tells her mother that she is going out with a friend to dinner and that she will be taking the kids with her. Her mother insists that they stay at home. As a result, Gerard and Teresa enjoy some time getting to really know each other.

He picks her up in his mother's car and asks her where she'd like to go for dinner. Teresa tells him that she is not into all that fancy stuff.

"I'll have a burger," she says. "Let's go to Alfie's."

Gerard thinks that she is teasing him, "You're playing, right? You can go there any day and everyday. Why now? Let me take you to a nice place, Teresa. I know a place you'll like. The food is really good."

After dinner, Gerard and Teresa sit and talk before leaving the restaurant.

Teresa inquires, "So what made you do this?"

"Do what?"

"What made you ask me to dinner? Why me?"

Gerard smirks and then shakes his head. "You act so surprised."

"Well, I don't date much. I don't really hang out much with anybody because I don't really make friends that well. I don't really try… It's hard for me to draw close to people."

"Why? You're so friendly I would've never thought that."

"Gerard, since we're friends now I can tell you this... I'm divorced. My husband was verbally and physically abusive, and he did a lot of damage to my self-esteem for a long, long time. He made me feel so bad about myself."

"I'm sorry to hear that... So you divorced him, huh?"

"I had to get away from him. Besides, I wasn't the only one, if you know what I mean."

"You mean he cheated on you?"

"He always did, and like a fool I married him, thinking that he'd change... Those kind of men never change. They just want you to believe they do until the next time when your lips end up swollen and busted up, or your eyes are black and blue. One night he came home drunk and became outraged because he didn't like what I fixed for dinner. I had to go to the hospital because he grabbed me by my hair and dragged me down the porch steps. I was all scraped up. He cracked one of my teeth when he hit me. I was a punching bag, Gerard. He didn't appreciate me at all. I married a monster, and I'll never do it again."

"Oh, everybody's not like that. There are plenty of good guys out there."

Teresa smiles at Gerard and remains silent for a moment. Then she speaks, "I hope so."

That night after dinner and a movie, Gerard takes Teresa home and tells her that he enjoyed the evening with her. She did likewise.

Stephanie is still having some problems in her marriage. She and Jason are not really communicating well. When he comes over to visit the children, they barely face each other. Their teenage son is deeply hurt by his parents' breakup and lashes out at them both.

"This is ridiculous! You've been together for so long and you can't even talk to each other! Why are you doing this? Why are you doing this to Allison and me? We're a family!"

Stephanie tries to pacify her son and places her arms around him. He pulls away and says, "Can't you even try to work this out? Don't you still care about each other?"

Jason looks away and then turns back around and says, "It's not that simple, son."

"It's just that simple! Yes it is!" Troy expresses. "I always thought that when two people love each other they stick together no matter what. You taught me that. Are you going back on your own words?"

Jason and Stephanie are embarrassed and do not know what to say. Troy leaves the room. After a few minutes, he leaves the house.

"Where are you going?" Stephanie inquires.
"Out."

Jason defends Stephanie, "Troy, your mother asked you a question. Where specifically are you going?"

"What do you care? You're never here anyway."

Jason grabs his son up by the collar and yells at him. "Listen to me, I know you're upset over this whole thing, but you will never have the right to disrespect me like that! You understand me?"

Troy begins to weep as his father lets him go. Jason realizes that Troy is suffering too, and that he and Stephanie are not the only ones. He and Stephanie look at each other and then both wrap their arms around Troy.

"Troy, what is going on between your mother and I has nothing to do with how we both feel about you. We love you and your sister very much. We're just going through a rough time right now. That's part of marriage—ups and downs. I care about your mother, and she cares for me too."

When Jason says this, Stephanie grins slightly at him. She has been feeling for weeks now that she and her husband were possibly headed for a divorce; however, to hear Jason acknowledge that he cares about her is comforting. That night, she asks him if he'd like to have dinner with her and the children. Jason kindly refuses and says, "I have a meeting tonight with one of my clients." Stephanie is somewhat disappointed but understands.

She replies, "Oh, okay."

Jason leaves. Just when Stephanie and the children sit down to begin their meal, Jason re-enters the house. Stephanie rises up from the table and asks, "Oh, you came back for your jacket, right? The jacket is hanging up on the rack."

Jason admits, "Well, I did leave my jacket and came back for it, but I decided to stay and have dinner with you all, if it's alright."

Stephanie cannot believe her ears. Jason wants to stay. Maybe this is a sign of reconciliation. She politely urges, "Pull up a chair. Let's eat."

Jason smiles at her and joins the rest of the family at the table.

Meanwhile, Keith's wife Cassandra is coming home from a friend's dinner party. Keith has some friends over at their home, and the driveway is full with their cars, so she attempts to park temporarily down the block.

As she opens the door to get out of the car, a man dressed in black comes out of nowhere and threatens her. "Get back in the car."

Cassandra is startled but does what he says. She cannot even see his face but notices a barrel pointed right at her. He has a gun. "Slide over into the passenger seat."

Cassandra is calm because she knows that any sudden move can mean her life. "What do you want?"

The man starts to drive away as Cassandra shakes her head, "No, no, please just take the car. Just take the car!" She assumes that the man is a carjacker.

"Shut up!" The man screams at Cassandra and continues to drive away, pointing the gun at her head. She tries to remain as calm as possible, but she starts to cry. The mysterious man starts a conversation with his victim. "I've seen you before... I've seen you many nights going into your house. Sometimes I could tell that you were alone."

Cassandra is shocked that this man has been stalking her. She tries to get a good look at his face, but he keeps his hood on and looks straight ahead as he drives. "Why are you doing this to me? Why me?"

"Because I like you, and you're pretty. I see you a lot in town."

"I have a family—a husband and three children. If it's money you want—"

"If I wanted your purse I would've taken it a long time ago. That's not what I want from you."

"Please, just don't take my life. I have a family."

"You've said that already. Besides, I won't kill you if you do what I ask you to."

The man continues to drive and eventually stops at a deserted parking lot across town. He wants to make sure that no one sees or hears what is going on. "Don't you try anything, lady. By the way, what's your name?"

"Cassandra—my name's Cassandra."

As the strange man steps out of the driver's side of the car, he says to Cassandra, "I will use this, so don't do anything funny. Understand me?"

Cassandra nervously nods her head. She is still sitting in the car wondering if she should make a move to escape. The man walks around to her side of the car and opens the door. She assumes that he wants her to get out; however, he orders Cassandra to just relax and that everything will be fine. She does not know what he means by this. "What are you doing?" She boldly asks.

The man slightly grins at her. She looks into his eyes as he moves closer to her body. He leans over right in front of Cassandra to the point where their chests meet and starts to twirl his fingers into her hair. Cassandra weeps uncontrollably as she stares down the barrel of a gun. She has few alternatives at this point and begs for the man to stop what he is doing to her. She screams several times as he muzzles her with his hand. After suffering a long, humiliating kiss down her neck, Cassandra courageously slithers her hand onto the gun and attempts to point it away from her, but the man is too strong and resists her efforts. He angrily slaps her with a backhand and places the gun on the driver's seat.

Cassandra screams, "Why are you doing this to me? Why?"

"Just shut up and relax! You're gonna make it worse for yourself! I'm warning you, Cassandra!" The man continues to be physical with his victim and ignores her bitter wailing. Cassandra has to smell his foul saliva on her face, neck and chest as he kisses her. His hands feel like poison on her skin as he rubs her body. To make matters the ultimate worst, the man tries to unbutton Cassandra's pants.

She resists and tells him, "No! No, please stop!" She then screams out again, "Somebody help me! Help me!"

Cassandra remembers that he has placed the gun on the seat and quickly struggles to grab it, but he is too fast for her and violently shoves Cassandra back onto the passenger seat. She scuffles with him, screaming at the top of her lungs and kicking him and punching him so that she can break free. The man is growing tired of his aggressive victim and starts to choke her. Cassandra tries everything that she can to free herself from this death grip, but she cannot. She cannot breathe well and starts to panic.

Almost out of breath, Cassandra is able to raise her knee sharply into his groin area. The man grimaces and collapses over onto the driver's seat. He is feeling excruciating pain and continues to hold his groin area. Cassandra makes a mad dash out of the car and runs for her life. It is unfortunate that she did not even get a chance to look at his face. All she can remember seeing is his eyes and thick eyebrows. It was too dark to recognize any distinctive features. She can remember no other details about the man.

Back home, Keith is becoming concerned about her, so he calls her friend to see if she is still at the dinner party.

"No, Keith, she left over an hour ago. Maybe she stopped somewhere else on the way home."

"Okay, thanks Melanie."

Keith tries to reach his wife on her cell phone, but it was left inside the car along with Cassandra's purse. As the phone rings, the man does not pick it up. In fact, he throws all of her belongings out of the car and carefully wipes away his fingerprints.

After a few attempts, Keith tells their daughter Chavonne that he finds it odd that his wife is not answering her phone. "It's late. I'm worried about her… I hope she's home real soon."

Later on, someone knocks at the door. It is a police officer. Keith is alarmed by this visit and asks, "What happened? Is it my wife?"

Keith is informed that Cassandra is at the police station filing a report.

"Filing a report? What happened? Is she alright?"

"Fortunately, she is alright now, sir. Your wife was raped a little over an hour ago. She's pretty shook up and bruised, but I think that she'll be okay once she seeks some medical attention."

Immediately, Keith is angry and hurt over his wife's ordeal. He feels awful and wishes that he had been there to prevent this from happening. He is too nervous to drive and accompanies the police officer back to the station.

When they arrive, Cassandra is just staring into space. She does not even notice him approaching until Keith places his hand on her shoulder. She quickly jerks away, not realizing at first that it is her husband.

"It's me, baby. It's me," Keith reassures. Cassandra bursts into tears as she rises up and embraces her husband. He takes her into his arms and tells her that everything is all right now. Keith starts to cry as he looks at his wife's battered face. He gently rubs it and says, "I'm so sorry. I'm so sorry this happened to you." They both cry uncontrollably.

A female police officer on duty is watching. She has to excuse herself from the room because it is just too much for her to watch. She mumbles to her partner, "Look at that lady's face. Look what she had to go through."

The other one says, "I'm just glad that she's alive."

Keith escorts Cassandra to the hospital and calls the family to let them know what happened to her. After the doctor cleans her wounds, he gives her a prescription for some pain medication and discharges the patient.

"She's pretty shocked by all this, Dr. Ross. I can't believe this happened to her. I just can't believe it."

That night after returning home, Chavonne tries to comfort her mother by giving her a hug. "Mom, I'm so sorry." Chavonne starts to cry, "I'm so sorry for you."

Keith tells his daughter to make her mother a cup of warm tea. Chavonne goes into the kitchen to make the tea. As she turns back around to watch her father console her mother, she accidentally drops the glass container of sugar onto the floor. Her father turns around and gets up to help her. He assumes that Cassandra will just rest on the sofa; however, when he returns, she is not there.

"Cassandra?" he calls, but she does not answer. As Keith walks down the hallway, he enters their bedroom. Cassandra's clothes are scattered on the floor in a trail leading to the bathroom. For a moment, he just stands there and watches his wife shower. He can see her through the glass door vigorously scrubbing her body. He is not sure whether to leave her like this or to assist her. "Cassandra, are you okay in there?"

She does not answer him at first. As Keith turns to walk away, she replies, "His breath, his breath smelled so awful. It smelled like beer." Keith turns back around and re-enters the bathroom. Cassandra continues to speak, "By the time I got to the police station, his saliva had dried up on my neck. His breath smelled like beer. Can you imagine what it feels like to have your dignity stripped away from you? He pointed a gun at me and made me just sit there while he used my body for his pleasure. I begged him, Keith, I begged him so many times to stop!"

As Cassandra becomes fueled with anger, Keith begins to fall apart. He cannot keep his composure and starts to weep again as he listens to his wife describe her terrible ordeal.

"He even asked me my name, as if that would somehow make us friends or pacify me. He tried to unbutton my clothes and had the audacity to tell me to relax. How could I relax? You know what? I didn't even see his face. I can't even identify him in a line-up. If I saw him on the streets again, I wouldn't even know that it was him... I have nothing... I can't do a single thing. He's coming back here. I just know he will. He told me that he could always tell when I was here alone. That scares me, Keith. I'm really scared."

"We'll find him," Keith confidently replies. "He won't get away with this."

For weeks, Cassandra finds it hard to get back into her rhythm. She is uneasy and jittery most of the time. The children notice a change in their mother, but they understand that she has suffered through a tremendous ordeal. She is also afraid to be alone in the house. Someone always has to be with her, particularly her husband. Cassandra feels safe and secure with Keith being around her. Every night, she falls asleep in his arms. He does everything that he can to make her feel confident in her home environment.

His younger brother Robbie calls to check on Cassandra.

"So how is she doing these days?" Robbie inquires.

"Well, she's trying to cope with it, but it's hard. It's hard for me too, Robbie. Over a period of weeks, I have watched my wife literally scrub the skin on her body until it starts to peel. Yesterday I had to step into the shower with her and make her stop scrubbing. In her mind, he has contaminated her body. Can you imagine how she feels having her body violated in such a way? All Cassandra could think about was just getting away from him, and he just made her sit there as he pointed a gun to her head… He could've killed my wife—just like that. He could've killed her, and then I would have to spend the rest of my life suffering without her." Keith starts to cry as Robbie sighs.

"I'm so sorry that she went through all of this. I know that you can't erase all of this and make things perfect, but you must know that you are making a difference just being there for her. She needs you."

"I can't leave her side for long without her becoming nervous. I haven't worked in three weeks consecutively. It's rough man. It's rough. She's not working, of course. Before long, our account will be drained. Chavonne has already asked me if she can get a job, but I said no because I want her to concentrate on school. My daughter has worked too hard for too long to get sidetracked now. If I have to work another job, then I will."

"What about Cassandra?"

"Well, we'll just have to work something out. Maybe Mama can keep her company when I'm not here."

"Listen Keith, I want to help you."

"You don't have to do that, man. It's not your responsibility."

"You're my brother, and I love you. Let me help you. I'm in a position to do this, so let me do it. Stop being so proud and let people do things for you sometimes."

Robbie sends his older brother a check for $2,000 to help alleviate some of the financial strain. It is greatly appreciated.

Keith has a talk with his mother. "Mama, I know that you have things to do, but I really need a favor from you. Cassandra is still afraid to be alone. I totally understand that, but the problem is the financial part of this. I haven't worked in almost three weeks, and I don't want to lose my job. We need the money. What I'm asking is that maybe you could talk to her. Maybe I'm not saying the right things to my wife. She probably needs a woman's perspective."

"I'll see what I can do... Keith, just be patient with her. She needs you more than anybody else right now. You're her husband, and this is a time when she really needs you more than ever to be her very best friend. Just love her and take care of her as you always do."

"I'm trying, Mama. I just hate to see our lives so upside down like this. I hate to see her so afraid. That's not Cassandra. She's a strong woman, and I just want her back the way she was. I know it'll take some time. I love her, and I'll do whatever it takes to help her... I'm not going to try and rush her back to work because she may not be ready, but I need to work. Is it possible that you could come over during the day and just sit with her a while? She needs some company. She says it's too quiet in the house when she's alone. She can hear a pin drop."

Mrs. Glover agrees to keep her daughter-in-law company for a while during the day, and this gives them even more of an opportunity to bond. They are already close, but their relationship is strengthened at this point.

In the meantime, Gerard is falling head over heels for his co-worker Teresa Valdez. He goes to a jewelry store one evening after work and purchases a diamond-clustered brooch for her. He shows up at her doorstep with a smile on his face. He knocks, and she opens the door. Teresa's smile indicates that she is happy to see him.

"Hello, come on in."

"Thank you."

"So you just got off work?"

"Yeah, about an hour ago... Teresa, I have something for you." Gerard reaches into his pocket and takes out a box. He gives it to her.

Teresa opens the box and is very surprised. She looks up at Gerard and expresses, "It's beautiful. Thank you, Gerard. Thank you very much."

"I'm sure that you have some pretty dress in your closet to wear with it."

Teresa smiles and replies, "No, but I'll get one."

She gives Gerard a hug and asks him, "I really do appreciate the gift, but if you don't mind me asking, what is the reason for this? Did I do something special that I don't know about?"

Gerard blushes and says, "It's just something I wanted to do for you—just for you being special like you are. Stop second-guessing things all the time."

Teresa believes that Gerard is just too good to be true. She stands there in front of him and shakes her head.

"What? What it is, Teresa?"

"It's just that you came out of nowhere, and you just know how to say all the right things and do all the right things. How could you be so perfect?"

Gerard realizes that he is not as perfect as his friend thinks. He feels somewhat guilty because Teresa does not know some of the trouble he has been in. He is attempting to turn over a new leaf and be around someone positive like her. Gerard is falling in love with Teresa. That evening, he takes her and her children out to dinner. Teresa's son Angel likes Gerard. In fact, Teresa has to squeeze in a conversation with Gerard because her son is so talkative with him. She is glad to see her son open up to Gerard. Her daughter is five-year-old Marisa. She smiles a lot and does not say too much. She is sort of shy. The evening is wonderful until Gerard spots one of his old street buddies, Victor. Immediately his countenance falls, and Teresa notices.

"Is something wrong, Gerard?" she asks.

"Umm, everything's fine. I'm alright." He continues to converse with her and tries to pretend that he did not see Victor. To his surprise, Victor approaches them at their table. Teresa can sense a bad vibe between the two men.

Victor speaks, "Good evening, how are you?"

Teresa responds, "Fine, and yourself?" She looks down into her plate and starts nervously picking her food with the fork.

"Hello, Jerry, what's up, man?" Victor uses a nickname for Gerard.

"Hey Victor, how ya doing?"

Victor can tell that Gerard really does not want to talk to him, but he pushes the conversation further to the point where Gerard excuses himself and goes outside with Victor. Teresa wonders what this is all about. She has never seen Gerard so nervous before.

"Why did you do that, man?" Gerard asks.

"Do what?" Victor replies.

"You came over there and interrupted my date."

"Oh, my bad. I'm sorry, man. I just haven't seen you in a while. You a family man now? Does she know you like I know you? Does that woman know that you used to snatch purses from old ladies?"

"I'm not like that now, Victor. Look, I gotta go. She's probably wondering what I'm doing out here. I gotta go."

Victor presents an enticement. "I got something good man, something real good you might be interested in being a part of."

"No, I'm not interested."

"You don't even know what it is."

"I gotta go, man. See you round."

Gerard starts to walk back in the door as Victor says, "Look, I know you're trying to impress your girl and all that, so I'll get with you later."

"Victor, I told you I'm not interested. I don't owe anybody money, and I'm not pushing no more drug deals. I gotta stay away from that stuff. I'm a 42-year-old man who has nothing to show for his life but wasting it. My own family doesn't even believe in me. I have to prove that I'm worth something, and I have a nice lady in my life now. For once in my life I'm trying to do something right. I can't mess that up. I just can't."

When Gerard returns to the table, Teresa is concerned. "You don't look so good. What did that guy say to you?"

"He's just an old buddy. We used to hang out together, that's all." Gerard changes the subject, but Teresa still has doubts that he is okay. She knows that something went wrong between Victor and Gerard. However, because he deliberately changed the subject, she leaves it alone.

After Gerard takes Teresa and her children home, he heads home himself. He is worried about bumping into Victor again. True enough, two days later Gerard is coming home from work when Victor approaches him. "I told you I'd catch you later. I meant that, man... So you in?"

Gerard firmly states, "No! I'm not in anything! Leave me alone, will you?"

Victor aggressively reminds Gerard of something. "Remember you said that you didn't owe anybody money? You're a liar, because you owe me. Remember? We were supposed to go half and half on that deal—"

"That was a long time ago, Victor!"

"Yeah, but I remember it like yesterday. You bailed out and made yourself disappear for a while."

"I was in jail, man."

"Yeah, well you're out now. Cough up the money you owe me. No, I tell you what you can do. I'll set this deal up for you, and you can work it off. It'll be like you're my employee. How's that?"

"I don't want any part of this, Victor."

"Let me do some math here, Jerry. If you owed me $2,500 three years ago, let's see how much interest you've piled up on yourself."

"I don't have $2,500 to give you!"

"Oh, you really owe more than that. I charge interest for slip-ups like the one you pulled." Victor slowly pulls out a gun from his pocket and points it at Gerard's stomach. "I'd hate to put a hole in your gut."

Gerard does not try to be a tough guy. He complies with Victor's wishes and asks, "What do you want me to do?"

"First, let's have a drink for old time's sake. Three years is a long time to not see my good ol' buddy. Let's go get a drink. We got a lot to talk about."

Just when Gerard thought that his life was slowly coming together, an old buddy comes around to mess it up. Gerard has not seen Victor in three years, and he was hoping for them not to meet again. He does owe Victor money and wants to settle the issue between them so that he can walk away with a clean slate. This is the last thing that he needs to be a part of, considering the fact that he is attempting to be a better person. Nevertheless, Gerard sees no other alternative but to go through with this. He knows that Victor Lindsay is a dangerous man who means what he says and does even more.

That night, Victor treats Gerard to a few drinks. He is so preoccupied with what he has chosen to do that he forgets that he is scheduled to work the next day. Gerard had initially agreed to cover a shift for someone else, and he himself neglected to show up for work. Mr. Douglas gives him a call.

"Gerard, this is Mr. Douglas. Did you forget that you were supposed to come in this morning for Joe? You volunteered to do it last week, remember?"

"Oh, I'm sorry. I did forget... Listen Mr. Douglas, I have to admit that I'm not really feeling my best this morning. I'm sick."

Mr. Douglas replies, "Well, I guess if you're sick then you can't work... Just come in tomorrow, okay? Don't forget that you're scheduled for tomorrow afternoon at three."

"I'll be there," Gerard confirms.

Mr. Douglas hangs up, and Gerard taps himself on the head and murmurs, "I'm messing up now. I'm messing up." For hours, he just sits in his room and stares at the wall. He cannot believe what he has gotten himself into. When he comes out of his room, Mrs. Glover is surprised to see him.

"I thought you were gone to work."

"No, I didn't go in this morning."

Since she doesn't seem to notice anything wrong with him, Mrs. Glover asks her son, "What's wrong? Are you sick? You didn't quit, did you?"

"No Mama, I didn't quit. I'm just taking today off, that's all. I go in tomorrow afternoon."

"Oh, okay. You want some breakfast? I'll make you some pancakes."

"I'm not hungry, Mama. I just need some time to myself."

Later that evening, Teresa stops by to see Gerard. She learned at work that he did not come in and wanted to make sure he was okay. When she arrives, Mrs. Glover greets her.

"Hello Teresa, come on in. Please, have a seat."

"Thank you, Mrs. Glover."

"I'll get Gerard for you. He'll be right out." Mrs. Glover goes down the hall and tells Gerard that Teresa is there.

"Hello Teresa, how are you?" Gerard greets her.

"Fine. I was concerned when I didn't see you today. Is everything okay? Are you sick? I can pick up a few things for you if you need me to."

"No that's not necessary, but thank you… I'm not sick, Teresa."

"Then what is it?"

"I'm just having a bad day, that's all. I just need some time to sort some things out. I'm just not feeling my best right now."

Teresa boldly asks, "Is this about us? Did I do something wrong?"

"Of course not! Why would you think like that?"

"I kind of got the feeling that you weren't too happy to see me just now… If you need my help or want to talk about something, you can trust me. I care for you—a whole lot. Don't shut me out now, Gerard. You convinced me to open up to you, and I did. I haven't done that in a long time with anybody. I saw something special in you."

Gerard tells Teresa, "Stop worrying so much. You and me are fine, okay?"

Teresa feels as though something is wrong with Gerard. She does not understand his behavior and is convinced that he is hiding something from her.

As Teresa says goodbye to Gerard, he speaks, "Wait." She turns back around, and he gives her a kiss on the cheek. She smiles and gently places her hand on his face. Gerard gives Teresa a hug.

"I'll see you later, Gerard."

"Okay," he replies.

Later that evening, Mr. Bartholomew stops by to see Mrs. Glover. He greets her with a dozen red roses. "Hello darling, how was your day?"

She replies, "Wonderful, just wonderful... These are lovely roses, Bartholomew."

"I'm glad that you like them. Are you ready for dinner?"

"Yes, one moment, please."

Mrs. Glover goes down the hallway and knocks on Gerard's door. "Gerard, I'm leaving now. I'll be back later on. There's plenty of stuff in the fridge for you to eat. There's leftover chicken, some cold cuts, and some apple pie."

He smiles and gestures for his mother to go away, "Mama, are you still here?"

Mrs. Glover grins at her son's comment. "Well, I can take a hint," she replies.

When his mother leaves, Gerard prepares to meet for the deal that Victor set up. After waiting at the location for about fifteen minutes, Gerard sighs and mumbles to himself, "What am I doing? I have to get out of here."

Just then, Victor sneaks up out of nowhere and tells him, "You did the right thing by showing up." Gerard is not in agreement with Victor's statement, but he does not walk away. He just wants to get this whole thing over with.

"Victor, I'm telling you right now that after I do this, I don't want you 'popping up' anymore around me. I want you out of my life for good. Is that understood?"

Victor pretends to feel insulted but subtly grins. "I think I can manage." He spots a black car and says, "That's them. That's who we're meeting."

Gerard never thought to ask Victor this before. "Why did you want me to be a part of this anyway? You could've done this yourself without me."

Victor's reply humiliates Gerard, "First of all, I wanted to see if you'd really go through with it. Word on the street is that you're soft now."

"You did this to test me!" Gerard angrily concludes.

"Why not? I haven't seen you in three years. I just wanted to see if you were still the same guy. Besides, you know my other reason. You ran off with my cut of that money three years ago, and that wasn't cool. You played me, and when I saw you again, I just had to jerk you around a little bit. There you were at a restaurant with your girl trying to be a family man, but I knew the real Gerard. I just had to try you one more time, and you went along with it."

"You had a gun! What else was I supposed to do?"

Victor is confident that he has the upper hand. He feels that he has weakened Gerard. In a sick, twisted way, he feels a sense of satisfaction and control.

Gerard goes through with the drug deal and hears a police officer tell him, "You're under arrest." Victor and Gerard were under arrest. They did not know that the other party was two undercover cops that had been watching Victor over a period of time. They needed to have proof of what he had been doing, and now they had it. It is unfortunate for Gerard that he is a part of this.

When Mrs. Glover arrives at the city jail Keith, Cassandra, and Mr. Sanders accompany her. She has been crying. Keith is very angry with his brother, but even more hurt over the fact that Gerard messed up a chance to get his life together.

"I just feel like choking him, Mama."

Mrs. Glover does not reply, but Cassandra nudges Keith and murmurs, "Honey, your mother doesn't need to hear you say that."

When the warden gives Gerard the opportunity to speak with his family, he only wants to talk to his mother. He feels a deeper sense of commitment to her because she was so proud of the changes that he had made, and she had verbalized this. Gerard knows that he has hurt her deeply by this setback. It is hard for him to even look her in the eyes, but he tries.

"Mama, I'm glad you came… There are really no words that can explain what I'm feeling right now."

"What you're feeling? How do you think the rest of us feel right now, to know that you're in here?"

"I know that I cheated you—"

"You cheated yourself, Gerard. You're a 42-year-old man who has nothing. You're an empty person with an empty heart. You're just rotten to the core."

Gerard has never heard his mother speak to him in such a way before. His feelings are deeply hurt by this. "Mama, I tried."

"Well, it wasn't good enough! Why couldn't you do something productive with your life like your brother Keith—"

"I knew it. I just knew that eventually you would go there!"

"Don't you shout at me, boy! You're always putting Keith down and belittling Robbie, but deep down I know that you're just jealous of what they've accomplished in their lives! You're always making excuses for yourself and the things you do. Well, I've had it, Gerard. Do you hear me? I have had it with you!"

"Mama, I promise you that once I get out of here, I'll do better, and this time I'm not going to mess up. I promise."

"No more promises, Gerard, because your promises turn into lies. Don't lie to me, son."

Gerard assumes that his mother is going to bail him out of jail, but she does not.

"You're just going to let me stay in here? How could you? I told you why I did this whole thing, Mama. Victor set me up. He pulled a gun on me. What was I supposed to do?"

"Why didn't you just tell somebody about this so they could help you? You make it seem as if there was just nothing else for you to do but go and sell some drugs to a cop. You make it seem as if there was no other alternative."

"If I had come to the police with this, do you think they would've actually helped somebody like me, who already has a record?"

"Well, what you chose to do certainly didn't make things better, did it? I believed in you, Gerard, and you made a fool of me. You took advantage of me because I'm your mother, and you know that I love you. You always think that you can just run back into my life after you mess up. You think that way because I made it easy for you to do, but not anymore. You're on your own now—for good."

Gerard does not understand what his mother is implying. "What are you saying, Mama?"

Mrs. Glover starts to weep as she continues speaking to her son, "I love you Gerard, but you've really proven yourself to be a disgrace to me and your whole family. For most of your life I've watched you do everything but what was right, and it just breaks my heart to see you continue with this course. I imagine you're going to your grave being a man without real purpose. As I said before, you're empty. You have nothing to give anybody else because you didn't do anything right for yourself… Until you get yourself together, I don't want you around me. As a matter of fact, you probably won't get yourself together since you've messed up so much before. I don't want to see you. I'm done."

Gerard starts to shake his head in disbelief. He cannot believe that his mother is abandoning him. He cannot bear the pain. "No, Mama, you don't mean that."

"Yes, I do. Your father and I were good parents, but you didn't appreciate anything that we taught you about being a man… I'm sorry you turned out like this. It just breaks my heart. Goodbye, Gerard."

"Mama! Mama, you can't mean this!" Gerard shouts as his mother makes a tearful exit from the room where they conversed. Mrs. Glover is heartbroken. Gerard bangs on the table in anger. He cannot believe that his own mother has cut him off. Now he realizes the magnitude of his actions and how much he has lost in the process.

The next day Mrs. Glover is getting out of her car when Teresa Valdez approaches her. She is curious about Gerard.

"Hello Teresa."

"Good evening, Mrs. Glover. I stopped by to see Gerard. Is he here?"

"No, unfortunately he's not."

"I heard at work today that he didn't show up again. I think they let him go."

"Teresa, Gerard is in jail."

Teresa is in shock. "In jail? For what?"

"He was busted for selling drugs to an undercover cop."

Teresa sighs in disbelief and shakes her head. "No, this doesn't make any sense. Why would he do this?"

"Teresa, my son has a past that eventually got the best of him. I thought he had changed."

"I can't believe what I'm hearing… This doesn't even sound like something that he would do."

Mrs. Glover observes, "You care for him a lot, don't you?"

"Yes, I do. This really is a hard pill for me to swallow, Mrs. Glover. Gerard and I are close. I would've never imagined something like this… I would like to see him, though. I really need to talk to him."

Teresa visits Gerard. He is happy to see her, but somewhat ashamed.

"Your mother told me what happened. Gerard, how could you do this? I can't believe that I'm standing here looking at you in a jail cell, and just the other night we were out having dinner with my kids. I don't really know you like I thought. I set myself up for this. I should've known that any guy to ever walk into my life only means disappointment."

"Don't say that. I care about you, Teresa."

"You lied to me!"

"No, I didn't lie to you. Everything that I have ever said to you was true, Teresa."

"Well, you conveniently left out a few details!"

"Teresa, I couldn't tell you about my past!"

"Why not?"

"Because I didn't want to lose you!" Gerard admits. "You think that I wanted to tell you that I used to be out there on the streets day in and day out pushing dope and doing all kinds of stuff? If I had done that, you would've never given me a second look. You know that!"

Teresa does not know what to say at this point. She turns her back to Gerard. He feels terrible and wishes that he could say the right thing to make Teresa feel better. He knows that she is hurt, especially when she starts to cry.

"No, please don't start crying. I can't take it. The last thing in this world that I would want to see is you crying. I didn't mean to hurt you. I love you."

Teresa turns around and faces Gerard. She replies, "I just have to know why you did this. I have to know why you messed up like this."

"Do you remember the guy that we saw at the restaurant?"

"Yes."

"Well, he and I had a past. As I said before, we were street buddies. We got into a lot of stuff together, but one time I decided to be greedy and take off with some money that I was supposed to split with him. That's why when I saw him that night he was so persistent. He had not forgotten what I did."

"So you teamed up with him again for one last run?" Teresa sarcastically questions.

"Not exactly. He used our little 'money problem' to get back at me. I was suckered into the drug deal, and it turned out to be two cops that had been on his trail without him knowing it. I just got caught right in the middle of it."

"I wish that you weren't 'caught' in the middle of anything. I could tell that night that something wasn't right with you and that guy. I just sensed it right away, but you told me that you were all right. That's why I dropped the issue. Maybe if I'd been a little bit more of a nag you would've opened up to me and said more about it... I can't believe that I let myself fall for you. Every time that I meet someone, I always tell myself that this time it's going to be right, but it never is."

Gerard reassures, "Teresa, I didn't want to do this. Maybe I didn't handle myself the right way or make the best decision, but you gotta believe that I didn't want to do it. I really didn't want to. When I started working at the supermarket, at first I only did it to stop my mother from complaining. Initially I did it for her, but I realized that it was the right thing for me to do in order to get back on track. For once, I was happy with my life and didn't have to look over my shoulder because of doing anything wrong. I had a good conscience, I was making a living, I had gained my mother's confidence and I met you. I had something to live for, and that made me feel good."

"But look how easy you risked everything. Now you're back where you started, and I can't trust you. I can't trust you, even though I want to. I can't trust you with my kids. What kind of example would you be for them? I can't do this."

Gerard places his hands on Teresa's shoulders and tells her, "Listen to me clearly. I love you, and I never meant to hurt or deceive you. If I had never met up with Victor, then none of this would've happened. I just made a bad choice, and I'll have to pay for it. I understand the consequences of what I've done, but I really need you in my corner, Teresa. I need you to understand that I'm not this horrible person. I did change. I did try. My intentions were good. If it takes me the rest of my life to prove myself to you and my family, then I will. That's just what I'll do. Just don't shut me out. Remember you asked me not to do that to you? Remember?"

"I remember, but it's not the same thing Gerard. This is totally different than what I said the other day."

"I need you. I don't have anybody else right now. My own mother told me that she wants to have nothing to do with me. I don't think she really means it, but I know that I've really done some damage to our relationship for her to even say something like that. It's killing me to know that she has given up on me... I guess I can't blame her, though. She gave me every chance in the world, and I blew it every single time."

"So you want me to be loyal to you because no one else is?"

"I want you in my life—that's what I want."

Teresa is confused right now. She does love Gerard, but she doubts him. Teresa tells Gerard that she loves him very much but that she cannot continue being with him. He begs her to not give up on him, but she leaves him standing alone. Gerard sits down at the table and bursts into tears. He has lost everyone that means anything to him.

The following Monday morning, Cassandra does something that surprises Keith. He turns over to tell her good morning, but she has already gotten out of bed. She is in the shower preparing to go to work.

"Are you sure that you're ready, honey? Don't go if you're not ready."

Cassandra tells Keith, "All this time I've sat here in my house feeling paranoid and bitter over what happened to me. I can't spend the rest of my life like this. What that man did to me is something that I cannot change, but I can pick up the pieces and go on. He did that to control me, Keith. Don't you see it? That's what rapists do. They like to control people and play with their minds. I must admit, he has done some damage, but he cannot control my life. He doesn't have that right. This is my life, and I'm reclaiming it right now."

Keith smiles at his wife and takes her into his arms, "I love you."

"I love you too. Keith, I want to thank you for supporting me through this."

"Honey, you're my wife. It couldn't have been any other way as far as I'm concerned."

"I just wanted to let you know how much I appreciate you and how you keep this family together."

"Well, I couldn't have done any of this by myself. You have kept this family just as strong as I have, probably more. I realize sometimes that I'm overly concerned with providing for the family's material needs, but you have been an anchor of support in fulfilling the emotional needs of everyone in this house. You always know what to say to make things better for the kids and for me. Lately when I saw you so depressed, it broke my heart because I knew that you were suffering. I knew that you were a much stronger person than that...I'm so glad that you're feeling better. I'm going to do everything that I can to keep you strong because you've certainly made me stronger. I don't know what I'd do without you."

"I love you, Keith. You're everything to me."

Keith kisses his wife's lips and embraces her before she leaves for work.

Eventually, Mrs. Glover has some time to think about what she said to Gerard. He deeply hurt her, and she feels betrayed because she placed so much trust in him. One day Robbie calls home, and she expresses to him how she has been feeling. "I think I may have been too hard on him. I said some awful things."

"Mama, he hurt you. Don't feel guilty for standing up to Gerard. He's had every chance in the world to do better, but he always chose to do something else. He's just paying for it now."

"He's out of jail, but I don't know where he is. I haven't seen him. It's been months now." Gerard's absence is taking its toll on Mrs. Glover. She cannot eat and gets very little sleep. She feels guilty for cutting him off, but she tries to reason within herself that he will eventually come home. However, he does not return home this time.

Mr. Sanders notices a change in Mrs. Glover and expresses concern, "Sweetheart, I'm worried about you. I know that you miss your son, but your life is falling apart now. You're so unhappy these days. I wish that I could just make you smile or laugh again."

"I miss him, Bartholomew. I feel as if somebody just came along and ripped my heart out. I love my son. He may not be everything that I want him to be, but he's still my son. I'll never excuse his wrongdoing, but I'll never stop loving him either. I'll never forget how to be his mother. I wish that I could tell him that."

Mr. Sanders has a private conversation with Keith concerning his mother. "Keith, your mother is very worried about your brother. She feels guilty about what she told him that day when she visited him in jail."

"I don't know why. I wanted to say worse than that to him, but he only wanted to talk to her. I'm so angry with him. That good-for-nothing Gerard is just not worth any of our time. I don't care if I ever see him again."

Mr. Sanders doubtfully replies, "Somehow I don't believe that, Keith. I think that deep down inside, you really love your brother. You're just disappointed in him, that's all. If you didn't care about him, you wouldn't be so angry over what he's done."

Keith doesn't deny that he cares about Gerard. "You know, when we were kids he looked up to me. We were so close. I was proud of him, and he was proud of me. We looked out for each other. Nothing or nobody could come between us. We weren't just brothers. We were best friends. Gerard started hanging with the wrong kind of people as we got older, and he never left that lifestyle behind. I just figured that he was being young and silly and that eventually he would come out of that okay, but he didn't. He never learned better... Mr. Sanders, you can read me like a book. You could tell that I was worried about him. You really have been there for this family, and I want to thank you. At first I had my doubts, but you're a good man. That's not hard to see."

"That's quite a compliment, Keith. Thank you."

"More than anything, I've seen the way you reached my mother. When my father died, she was so sad. The love they had was incredible, and it hurt me to see her so sad even though I was suffering too. Since you've been in her life, my mother has been happier than I've seen her in a long time. It's as if you've revitalized her."

"Well, I love your mother. In fact, I wanted to propose marriage to her, but I'm afraid that this is not the right time for it, considering the situation with your brother. Marguerite is so depressed over Gerard that I don't want to do anything inappropriate. I guess that the best thing I can really do right now is be there for her."

Keith is impressed with the sincerity of Mr. Sanders towards his mother. He knows that Mr. Sanders truly loves his mother and wants to make her happy.

Mr. Sanders adds, "It would also mean a great deal for me to have your blessing on this. I know that you and your mother are very close, and what you feel is important to me. I hold your feelings in high regard."

Keith smiles at Mr. Sanders and says, "You don't have to get my consent to propose to my mother, but I appreciate your consideration. I only want what's best for her, and I honestly didn't think that anyone was good enough for her or could measure up to my father. However, just watching you over a period of time has brought me to my senses. You're just what my mother needs, Mr. Sanders."

Meanwhile, Stephanie and Jason are trying to patch things up between them. They have been separated for quite a while now but are gradually reconciling. He spends the evenings with her and the children over dinner several times a week.

One Saturday evening, Jason thinks about what his wife said to him once about being more romantic. As he sits in his apartment, he decides to do something special for her. He orders a bouquet of red roses. When they are delivered, Stephanie is in the kitchen venting over a broken casserole dish. She is just about to sweep up the mess when the doorbell rings. The deliveryman states, "I have a delivery for Mrs. Mathis."

Stephanie immediately smiles and replies, "That would be me."

"Sign here, please," asks the deliveryman as he gives Stephanie the beautiful roses.

She takes them into the house and sets them on the table. There is a note attached that reads: 'Stephanie, I admire you. It's no secret... Love, Jason.' For a moment, she blushes like a teenage girl experiencing a crush. When Stephanie attempts to call Jason and thank him for the roses, he is not home. About an hour later, he arrives unexpectedly.

"Hello Stephanie, I can see that you received the roses. I hope you like them."

"Like them? I love them. They're beautiful. Thank you."

"You're quite welcome... I was thinking about you, so I thought I'd drop by."

"Come on in. You just caught me in the middle of sweeping up the pieces of my casserole dish. It was a gift from one of our friends. I was being clumsy, and it fell off of the counter." Stephanie makes her way back into the kitchen to pick up the shattered dish as Jason follows.

"So where are the kids?"

"Oh, Chavonne took them to go see a movie. I'm here by myself cleaning. Eventually I will cook, once I get this mess cleaned up."

"Let me help you," Jason offers. As he kneels down with his wife to clean up the mess, he reveals, "I've missed you. I've missed you a lot, Stephanie... I've been wanting to come home for quite a while now."

"Why didn't you say something sooner?" she inquires.

"For starters, I've been observing the way you're able to manage without me. I was beginning to think that you were sort of getting used to me being gone."

"That's ridiculous, Jason. I've had it rough too. I just didn't show it. I try to be strong for the kids...but I've missed you terribly. Every night I wish that you were here. I can't even remember half of the stuff we've argued about over the past few months. All that matters to me—in fact, all that ever mattered to me in the first place is not losing you, Jason. You were here everyday, but it was as if your mind was somewhere else. You didn't seem to take interest in me anymore. That scared me."

"I'm sorry. I really am. A lot of times, I fall asleep on the sofa just thinking about how we got to this point. I did some self-examining, and I realized that I have taken you for granted for a long, long time. I took for granted what a wonderful, loving person you have always been. I got too caught up with everything else on the outside and forgot about what really mattered most to me— you and the kids. I really don't want us to stay apart like this. I've been a wreck."

"So have I. I don't want us to be like this either."

"Maybe I have been a bit arrogant. I got so mad because you told me that success had changed me and made me a different person. I didn't want to hear that. I always had the philosophy that success made a person better... It does make a person better if he stays focused, and I didn't do that very well."

"Jason, I talked a lot about what I wanted from you, but what do you want from me? What can I do to make this marriage work again?"

"I just want you to continue being the wonderful woman that you already are... Do you still love me like you used to?" Jason asks.

Stephanie replies, "Of course! I love you very much, Jason."

"Then that's all I need," he smiles. "I love you, Stephanie."

The couple continues to sit on the floor, talking. They have forgotten about the mess to clean up.

Jason and Stephanie try to rekindle the deep friendship that had always been at the core of their marriage. Jason moves back home and vows never to take his family for granted again. Being away from them made him realize just how empty his life could really be. He understood what his wife had been trying to tell him all along. During the separation Jason continued working hard and bringing in money for his company, sharing expensive dinners with colleagues and business partners and indulging in other luxuries; however, none of this seemed to mean as much in the absence of Stephanie and the children. At that point Jason felt like curling up in a "cardboard shack" with his wife just to be by her side. He remembered once that she used this expression to show the depths of her loyalty. It now made sense to Jason. Whether they had little or a lot, the family was better off together, not apart.

One evening, Mrs. Glover and Mr. Sanders go out to dinner. For the first time in weeks, she seems a little happier than she has been lately. As the couple enjoys their meal, the waitress asks them if they would like to finish their meal with a dessert.

"I wouldn't mind that," says Mr. Sanders, "Darling, would you like some dessert?"

"Oh, just a little bit of something—anything that you have," Mrs. Glover replies.

"Well, they have cheesecake, apple pie, chocolate cake, and peach cobbler," Mr. Sanders informs as he scans the menu. "What would you like, Marguerite?"

"The cheesecake will be fine."

"Okay," says the waitress as she leaves the table.

As the couple waits for their dessert, Mr. Sanders expresses himself. "I must say that I'm glad to see you feeling better. I've been worried about you, Marguerite. You've been so unhappy lately."

"I'm sorry."

"No need to apologize. I just like seeing you happy... I know that the situation with Gerard has taken its toll on you. I won't sit here and say that I understand what you're going through because I don't, but for what it's worth, I just want to let you know how much I love you and that I'm here for you."

Mrs. Glover is somewhat encouraged by Mr. Sanders words. They share their dessert and smile at each other, gazing into each other's eyes.

"Marguerite, I wanted to ask you something… In fact, I've wanted to do this for a while now, but the timing never seemed right until now… I'm not trying to replace your husband. I know that I cannot take his place, but I'm surely eager to bring some joy to your life and be your companion. Marguerite, will you marry me?"

Mrs. Glover is so surprised by the proposal that she nervously giggles and places her hand over her mouth. She did not expect this. Mr. Sanders patiently awaits an answer as Mrs. Glover regains her composure. She affirmatively answers, "Bartholomew, I will be your wife."

Mr. Sanders takes a small box from his pocket and opens it up. He places a beautiful diamond ring on Mrs. Glover's finger and reassures, "I love you."

Mrs. Glover hesitates at first, but then replies, "I love you too." At first, she feels sort of awkward telling another man (other than her late husband Charles) that she loves him. Nevertheless, she does love Mr. Sanders and cannot deny this. Since she has decided to marry the man, she must express her feelings to him. This moment is a milestone in the relationship.

The two tell their respective children the good news about the engagement, and they all are excited and happy for their parents. In fact, the two families decide to have dinner together so that they can get to know each other better. The event is one to cherish, as Mrs. Glover and Mr. Sanders watch their children socialize with each other. Everyone is caught up in the moment. Mr. Sanders places his arm around Mrs. Glover. As he smiles and glances at her, his countenance falls as he notices that she seems to be meditating about something. He is concerned.

"Are you okay, Marguerite?"

Mrs. Glover realizes that her fiancé can tell that she is not enjoying herself as much as she seems to be. She is thinking of Gerard, wishing that he were there to be with the rest of the family. He is like the missing puzzle piece.

To make matters worst unintentionally, Mr. Sanders' daughter Angela notices Gerard on a photo and asks, "Is this your son, Gerard?"

Mrs. Glover answers, "Yes, that's Gerard."

"Oh, it's such a shame that he isn't here. I was looking forward to meeting all of your family," Angela adds.

Mrs. Glover is now sad again. Angela does not realize what she has done. Keith notices his mother sort of drift away from the room for a while, so he goes after her while everyone converses.

She knows that it is her son behind her without even looking around. Keith places his hands on his mother's shoulders and kisses her cheek. "I love you Mama... I'm sorry about Gerard. Just for your sake, I wish that I could find him. I hate to see you like this. He just sucked the life right out of you."

"He didn't come back this time, Keith. Oh, he must know that I didn't really mean all those things I said. I was just angry, that's all. I was just angry. Now I can't change it... Here I am about to marry Bartholomew, and your brother isn't even here to celebrate with us."

"Do you love Bartholomew?"

"Of course, Keith. I would never marry a man that I didn't love. Why do you ask?"

"I just want you to be happy. I like Mr. Sanders. I can tell that he really does love you. I guess I just want to make sure that you are really okay with all of this and not just marrying him because he asked you to."

"You know me better than that, son. I know that lately I may not have seemed like myself, but I'm sure about this. Trust me, son."

Keith smiles at his mother and takes her into his arms. "Just as long as you're happy, I'm alright."

Mrs. Glover compliments her son, "Keith, I probably don't say this often enough, but I love you very much. You're not only my son, but you're my friend too. I'm so proud of you and the kind of man you are. You're a wonderful husband and father, and you always put your heart into whatever you do. You always give your best to everybody and everything you do. I appreciate you."

Keith's eyes well up with tears as he states, "Mama, thank you. That's good to hear... I've been so down on myself about losing my job and making less money. I even thought that I wasn't even saying the right things to my own wife when she got raped. I tried to make her feel better, and I thought that I was failing. She told me that I made a difference though, and now you're saying pretty much the same thing... That means a lot to me. I feel like a man again."

"You were never less than that," Mrs. Glover reminds her son.

Just then, Mr. Sanders notices that his bride-to-be has wandered off from everybody. He approaches her and Keith. "Is everything alright?" he inquires.

Keith smiles and pats Mr. Sanders on the back and replies, "Yes, everything's fine." Keith leaves the couple to themselves and rejoins the family.

Mr. Sanders gazes at Mrs. Glover and starts to blush slightly. He is truly a man in love. "It's wonderful to have our children here like this, isn't it?"

Mrs. Glover nods her head, "Yes, it is wonderful." She remains quiet after this and takes Mr. Sanders's hand. They continue to mingle with their children. That night after everyone else leaves, Mr. Sanders and Mrs. Glover sit and talk about what adjustments need to be made once they are married. The couple makes a mutual decision for Mr. Sanders to move into her home and sell or rent his home.

"So do you want a small wedding or something larger?" Mr. Sanders inquires.

"No, I don't want anything fancy. I just want to marry you," Mrs. Glover firmly replies. "As far as I'm concerned, we can get married at the courthouse."

Mr. Sanders smiles and replies, "I suppose so... Is that what you really want, to get married at the courthouse?"

"I'm fine with that, unless you want more."

"I don't object to that, dear. Perhaps afterwards we could take a honeymoon somewhere for a few days... Do you know that Betsy and I never got to have one?"

"You never got to go on your honeymoon? What a coincidence. Charles and I didn't, either."

Mrs. Glover and Mr. Sanders seem to be made for each other. At this point in both their lives, they are very happy to have found someone to love and spend time with. They have become best friends.

"Marguerite, I love you," Mr. Sanders expresses.

"I love you too," Mrs. Glover reiterates.

Robbie eagerly attempts to get to know Mr. Sanders better. He remembers seeing Mr. Sanders in the past long before anything happened between him and Mrs. Glover. Robbie and Mr. Sanders hit it off well.

"I must say that you've made my mother very happy, Mr. Sanders. She really does love you. In fact, I teased her yesterday and told her that she's doing much better than I am in the love department."

Mr. Sanders replies, "Oh yeah?"

"Definitely. I don't know what's wrong with me. My last girlfriend and I dated a long, long time, but I got scared and called it quits."

"Why?"

"Well, she wanted things that I didn't think I was ready for in the relationship. As we became more serious, I started seeing less of my friends and stopped doing stuff I had always enjoyed. I was afraid that this relationship with her was taking control over my whole life, and I felt that I needed to breathe again. She was a nice girl, though. Wherever she is, I hope that she's happy. Her name was Vanessa. We spent every weekend together. She would drop by my house and start cleaning up and cooking, ironing my clothes, washing my clothes and doing everything that a woman would do for the man she loves. To her, this was totally natural. She was just trying to take care of me. I guess I should've appreciated it, but at the time I looked at it as a sign that Vanessa wanted to get married. I thought she was trying to tell me something."

"Did she ever say to you that she wanted to get married?" Mr. Sanders inquires.

"No, she never did. Vanessa was just a good person who probably appreciated me more than I appreciated her."

"Did you love her?"

"I don't know," Robbie admits with embarrassment. "People are supposed to know stuff like that, right? I guess it wasn't meant to be, then."

"Well, it's best that you ended things if you had doubts... You'll find someone."

"I hope soon. Mr. Sanders, I'm 37 years old. I live alone in a 3-bedroom beach house. Some nights I just lie there thinking I'll be alone forever. I'm tired of being alone. It's so quiet sometimes at night... The architect who designed that house for me years ago is a friend. At the time, I loved being away from everything, but now I feel that I've secluded myself. My neighbors are an elderly couple whom I've never even had a conversation with in six years. We just wave at each other and go on. I guess what I'm trying to say is that I feel lonely, and maybe I've been too picky towards dating women in the past — not that I just want to settle for anybody that comes along. I just think that I may expect too much and end up finding something wrong with everybody that I meet. I actually miss all of the things that Vanessa was doing for me. At the time I felt stifled. I'm not even implying that I want her back specifically, but I wish that I had someone to cook me a nice meal like that or to care enough about me to do my laundry or iron my clothes."

"Well, like I said before, you'll find someone. You're a nice person, and you're bound to attract the right woman. She'll probably come when you don't expect it."

That night Robbie has dinner with Mr. Sanders and his children. Marvin Sanders is a 47-year-old electrical engineer. He is married with four children, including a set of twins. His wife Beverly is a pediatrician. Angela Sanders-Clark is a 45-year-old interior decorator/seamstress who is married to a dentist, Ryan Clark. The couple has two daughters. Carlton Sanders is a 38-year-old college basketball coach. His wife, Katrina, is a social worker. The couple has one son.

The evening is going well. Initially it is not hard to tell that Carlton is an outspoken, outgoing, in-your-face kind of guy. Nonetheless, he does not come across as being rude. He is just more assertive than his wife. During the course of the evening Robbie notices something that troubles him about Carlton and Katrina. He is sitting down on their sofa when he overhears Carlton tell his wife, "You can't do anything right, woman. I just don't understand you."

Robbie wants to pretend that he did not hear his future stepbrother speak so condescendingly to his own wife, but Carlton did.

"Carlton, could you just keep your voice down? We're not alone. People can hear you."

Carlton murmurs, "Nobody's out here." The couple is standing on their patio outside when this occurs. "We should've ordered food and had it delivered instead of eating that stuff you fixed."

"Everyone seemed okay with the food, Carlton. Why are you complaining?" Katrina defends.

"That meatloaf was so dry that I almost choked on it," Carlton insults.

Katrina angrily starts to walk away from her husband, but Carlton grabs her arm and begins to squeeze it. His behavior is so discreet that no one notices what he is doing to Katrina except for Robbie.

"You're hurting me," she passively states. Just then Robbie decides to take action. He cannot stand another minute of this and rises up from the sofa. He pretends to be coming outside to get some fresh air, but he is really there to prevent Katrina from being more insulted than she already has been.

"You know, this is a perfect view," Robbie states, as he walks outside onto the patio with Carlton and Katrina. Immediately, Carlton moves away from his wife and gives Robbie a fake smile. The smile can be interpreted as 'I hope he didn't see me do that.'

Carlton is uneasy at this point. He says, "Yeah, my wife and I come out here at night sometimes and look up at the stars. Right, honey?"

Katrina murmurs, "Yeah, sometimes."

Robbie stares at Carlton for a moment, making him feel more uncomfortable than he already is. Eventually Carlton runs out of words to say and excuses himself. He goes back inside the house and mingles with the rest of his guests. Katrina had her back turned to Robbie, but then she turns around. Just as Robbie is about to go back into the house, Katrina asks him a question.

"You saw what he did, didn't you?"

Robbie nods his head and admits, "I also heard what he said to you… I'm sorry."

"Don't apologize for my husband's behavior… Carlton likes controlling me. He gets a thrill out of it."

"Why do you put up with it? You're a social worker. You help people everyday, but you won't help yourself."

"What am I supposed to do?"

"Stand up for yourself. You're his wife, and you deserve his respect."

"You make it sound so easy, Robbie."

"It is easy."

"We've been married a long time, and we have our son to think about."

"I'm sure that your son wouldn't want to know that his father does this to you."

Katrina sighs in despair and shakes her head. "I'm going back inside."

She leaves Robbie standing outside on the patio by himself. Eventually he joins everyone back inside the house. For the rest of the evening, Mrs. Glover can tell that her son is not enjoying himself. When he takes Mr. Sanders home, he and Mrs. Glover ride back to her house hardly saying a word.

"Robbie, what happened back there at Carlton's house that made you act so funny? You became so quiet."

"I'm alright, Mama."

"You sure?"

"Yes, I'm sure… I want you to know that I'm happy for you. Mr. Sanders is a nice man, and I can tell that he cares about you."

"He is a wonderful person, and I do love him… I'm glad this is happening for me at this point in my life. I must say that it feels wonderful, absolutely wonderful."

Robbie smiles at his mother and places his hand over her hand. "I love you."

Mrs. Glover states, "I love you, too Robbie… So when are you going to give me a daughter-in-law?"

Robbie smirks, "Well, at the rate I'm going, it may never happen."

"You were dating somebody for a while, weren't you?"

"Her name was Vanessa. She was a good woman, but I let her get away. I felt stifled, but now I wish I had somebody like her in my life. Ever since breaking up with her, I haven't had one decent relationship."

The next day Robbie and Keith join Mr. Sanders's son Marvin to help him paint his shutters. Carlton shows up about an hour later. Katrina and their son Dimitri accompany him. They go inside the house with Marvin's family as Carlton comes outside.

"Hey man, what's up?" he says to his brother Marvin.

Marvin tells Carlton, "I would high-five you, but I got paint all over my hands now." As Marvin rambles on about his job Robbie and Carlton make eye contact. Not a word is spoken, but the tension is so thick it can be cut with a knife. Keith and Marvin do not notice this friction between Robbie and Carlton. As the four men paint and swap their life stories, Carlton still wonders if Robbie saw him mistreat his wife. His conscience is bothering him, but as always, he hides behind aggression.

After the paint job is done, Keith walks out to the utility shed with Marvin. Carlton and Robbie are alone, and this is one awkward moment.

Carlton boldly assumes, "I get the feeling that you don't like me very much, Robbie."

"Did you hear me say that?" Robbie replies.

Just then Katrina opens the back door and asks her husband and Robbie if they want something to drink. This is one of the warmest days of the summer, but Katrina is wearing a purple long-sleeve shirt. Robbie wonders if she is covering up something. Everyone else is wearing t-shirts, tank tops and shorts—typical summer wear.

When Katrina serves the lemonade, Carlton is in the shed with his brother Marvin and Keith. Robbie asks her, "Are you alright?"

Katrina hesitates at first, but then she openly confesses, "He hit me last night when everybody left."

Robbie probes, "Is that why you're covered from head to toe in this summer heat?"

Katrina informs him, "My right arm is all banged up. I smashed a mirror with my arm when Carlton shoved me against the wall."

Robbie shakes his head in disbelief. He cannot believe that this woman can accept what her husband is doing to her. Just then, Carlton notices the two discussing something, and he casually walks over to join them.

"Hey, is that for me? Thanks, baby." He says this as he places his arm around Katrina and pretends to be the loving husband. Robbie does not buy this for one minute.

Carlton can sense Robbie's disdain for him. He realizes that Robbie must've witnessed what happened between him and his wife. Katrina goes back inside the house as Carlton asks Robbie to take a walk with him.

"I love Katrina."

"I beg your pardon?" Robbie questions.

"I love her, but sometimes she just gets under my skin. You ever had one of them?"

"No, I've never had a woman get under my skin so bad that I want to hurt her... I never had one of them. I never jerked any woman around or used her for a punching bag," Robbie replies. He is letting Carlton know that he saw what happened.

"You saw that little incident last night, huh? I figured that you had to since you've been giving me those dirty looks since last night. I could tell that you didn't like me. I can read people like a book."

"How could you hurt your own wife like that? How could you say that you love this woman?"

"I don't ever mean to do it. It just happens."

"I wish she had the courage to stand up to you man. Maybe if she did you'd back off."

Carlton is becoming agitated with Robbie giving him marital tips. "Listen to me—I know that your mother and my father love each other, but I don't bite my tongue for anybody. You don't have to like me. I don't really care about that. Just stay away from me and mind your own business. You got that?" Carlton says this with a shove to Robbie's chest. Marvin and Keith witness this and immediately intervene.

Before they can step between Robbie and Carlton, Robbie retaliates with a blow to Carlton's face. Marvin naturally defends his brother even though he saw Carlton shove Robbie. "What's going on over here?"

Robbie angrily shouts, "How did that feel to you, Carlton? Is that how hard you hit your wife when she burns your dinner or makes your meatloaf too dry like last night?"

Marvin waves his finger in Robbie's face and tells him to back off. Keith steps in and says, "It's not his fault anyway, man. You saw what Carlton did to him!"

Carlton's nose is bloody. Dimitri runs to the aid of his father. "Daddy!"

Katrina holds her son back and tells him to stay in the house. She questions, "What just happened out here?"

Keith speaks, "Your husband pushed my brother and got popped for it!"

Robbie can see a slight grin flash across Katrina's face as she turns her head to the left. It disappears just as fast as it appeared. She pretends to feel sorry for her husband, but Robbie knows that deep down inside, Katrina is not offended by his action towards her husband. Nevertheless, Katrina takes a napkin and wipes away the blood from Carlton's nose, since it appears to be the right thing to do. After all, she is his wife.

Keith and Marvin realize that Carlton is in the wrong; however, that sense of loyalty to one's brother seemed more instinctive at the time. Keith tells Robbie, "Let's go, man. Marvin, I'm sorry that this happened."

Marvin does not speak. He just raises his hand up and looks away as if he is implying, 'Let it go.'

Mrs. Glover and Mr. Sanders's children are on opposite sides of the fence now; however, the cat is out of the bag about Carlton's abusive behavior towards his wife.

Mr. Sanders is embarrassed to know that his son is like this. He never saw one clue of the abuse before. Keith and Robbie are concerned that their squabble with Mr. Sanders's sons will cause tension between the couple. As a result, Robbie humbly apologizes to him.

"Mr. Sanders, I apologize for hitting Carlton. He shoved me, and I just lost control. I wish that I had just walked away."

Mr. Sanders replies, "He started it. It's not your fault... That poor woman. I had no idea that Katrina was being hurt. If I had known about this, I would've spoken up and tried to help her. I'm so ashamed of Carlton. I didn't know that he was hurting his wife."

This incident puts a damper on things since Mrs. Glover is now having doubts about marrying into this family. Mr. Sanders is heartbroken and tries to persuade her.

"Marguerite, we can work through this."

"Bartholomew, our sons were about to beat the living daylights out of one another if Keith and Marvin didn't intervene. I just can't pretend that it didn't happen."

"Honey, what about us? Don't you love me, Marguerite?"

"Of course I do, Bartholomew."

"Then marry me. We can get past this! Please don't give up on me now! We've come too far!"

Mr. Sanders wants to call a truce between Robbie and Carlton in order to make things right between him and Mrs. Glover. The response he receives is shocking.

"Carlton, why don't you just apologize to the man for shoving him and be done with this? You were wrong, and you need to admit that."

"He had no right to stick his nose into my business!"

"Carlton, he saw you hurting your wife. Any caring, normal person cannot overlook something like that. Katrina loves you. Why do you treat her like this? You married this woman and promised to love and cherish her. You're not doing that by beating and insulting her. Maybe you two should get some counseling before this goes any further."

Carlton makes the ultimate mistake by giving his father an ultimatum. "Daddy, tell me that you're not still going to marry this woman after what happened."

"Why shouldn't I marry Marguerite? Why should I deny myself happiness with her just because of your stupidity?"

"If you marry that woman, then we have nothing else to say to each other." Carlton feels that by saying this that his father will give in, but Mr. Sanders remains firm.

"Carlton, how dare you try to intimidate me? I changed your diapers and made sure that you didn't go to bed hungry! Don't you dare talk to me like that! I'm your father no matter how old you are! I'm marrying Marguerite because I love her." Mr. Sanders leaves his son's home in anger.

When Mr. Sanders speaks with Mrs. Glover, she still displays some ill feelings over the situation between Carlton and Robbie. "Marguerite, I love you no matter what. We have no control over what happened between our boys."

"I just feel bad that our families don't get along now. I want to marry you, but I want all of us to get along."

"Marguerite, life isn't perfect, and people do things that are inappropriate sometimes. That's just how it is. You and me aren't responsible for the way they feel towards each other... I've talked to Carlton. I tried to convince him that apologizing to Robbie is the best thing to do."

"What did he say?" Mrs. Glover inquires.

Mr. Sanders replies with a deep sigh, "Well, he remained stubborn."

"You mean he didn't listen to you?"

"He told me that he won't speak to me again if I marry you. I think he's bluffing, though."

Mrs. Glover is very hurt by Carlton's remark to his father. She knows that she will not feel right marrying Mr. Sanders now that his son has given him such an ultimatum. She does not want their marriage to come between Mr. Sanders and his son. She starts to cry.

113

"Marguerite, what's the matter? Don't cry. What he said doesn't change the way I feel about you. I've already made my decision, and I'm sticking right beside you. I love my son, but he can't run my life. I won't tolerate that. Don't worry about Carlton."

"You just don't understand, Bartholomew. Don't you see that I can't marry you now? It just wouldn't be right to come between you and your son like this."

Mr. Sanders reassures her, "It's not your fault, Marguerite. I'll deal with my son, but marrying you is the best thing that I could do right now. I love you, and I want to spend the rest of my life with you. That's all I want right now. Please, don't give up on me."

"I love you, Bartholomew. That's why I'm doing this, because I love you so much. Even if you do marry me I know that you'll still be sad over your son. I just can't go through with this. I'm sorry."

Mr. Sanders is distraught over Mrs. Glover's decision not to marry him. He is deeply, truly in love with her and wants to be her husband. He sighs, "Why can't you see this any other way, Marguerite? You're breaking my heart... You're breaking my heart."

Mr. Sanders leaves Mrs. Glover's home with the saddest countenance. He feels lost and confused. Mrs. Glover is equally hurt by this sudden turn of events. One moment, things were going well between everyone. Suddenly, things just fell apart at the seams. Mrs. Glover becomes depressed and sad. To add to this pain is the fact that Gerard has not been around in months.

Gerard had drawn the conclusion that his family had given up on him for good this time and cannot bring himself to face them. He also misses Teresa. These days, Gerard sleeps at a shelter and receives three meals a day there. At night, he just meditates on all the things he has done wrong in his life. He does not like himself very much right now and feels ashamed that he has spent most of his life being a failure.

For days at a time, Mrs. Glover does not call anyone or even come out of the house. She is deeply upset over Mr. Sanders and Gerard's absence. Once the strong, rock-solid matriarch of her family, Mrs. Glover has weakened to the point of hopelessness and despair.

Mr. Sanders continues to take his dog for daily walks, but he cannot even bring himself to pass Mrs. Glover's home. He goes in the opposite direction and follows another path. They have had no contact since the night Mrs. Glover broke off the engagement. He has not spoken with his son Carlton either. It is such a shame that these two people developed a strong love for each other and it all came to an abrupt end because of the senseless actions of someone else.

Robbie feels partly responsible for the breakup between his mother and Mr. Sanders, but she sets matters straight. "Robbie, it's not your fault. I made the decision not to marry him."

"But it was because of me and Carlton."

"I said it's not your fault. Carlton told his father that if he married me he wouldn't speak to him again."

"What?"

"That's right. Carlton gave Bartholomew an ultimatum. He tried to talk his father out of marrying me simply because Bartholomew asked him to apologize to you. He stood up to Carlton, but I had to end the relationship because I can't stand to see Bartholomew and his son like this. Putting myself in Bartholomew's position, I couldn't imagine having a bitter relationship with any of you like that, so that's why I ended things... It hurts me so bad already to know that Gerard is gone because of something that I said. He must be pretty upset with me. I can't imagine seeing Bartholomew suffer like I'm suffering over your brother. I want him to make up with Carlton."

"Mama, you're punishing Mr. Sanders for what his son did. That's not fair. This man loves you. If he could stand up to his own son for your sake and my sake, then that should tell you something."

"I know that he loves me. I love him too, but I guess it's just not meant to be."

"Yes it is, Mama. Give that man another chance."

"No, Robbie, it's finished now."

One Saturday morning, Keith is about to take Cassandra's car to the body shop for a paint job. He sits in the driver's seat and attempts to adjust the seat when something small rolls from under it. Keith picks up what seems to be a pin-on employee badge. For a minute, he sits there in awe because he realizes what this could mean. He goes back into the house and asks, "Cassandra, do you know somebody named Todd?" He knows that she does not.

"No, I don't know any Todd."

"I found this in your car." Keith shows his wife the small employee badge with the name 'Todd' imprinted on it. They both realize that her rapist must have accidentally left it in the car because since the incident and recovery of the car, no other man besides Keith has been in Cassandra's car—certainly no man named Todd.

Keith grins slightly and says, "Well, at least we know his name now, and that he works at Bush's Sports Bar."

"We've got to report this to the police," Cassandra advises.

"We will, after I see him first for myself."

"Keith, don't go down there and do anything foolish. Don't mess this up."

117

"He's got to pay for what he did to you. We will go to the police, but this badge just isn't enough on its own to nail him. Even if the authorities question him, he can deny it. It will only be his word against yours. The next thing you know, he'll be off free walking the streets again."

"Don't play detective, baby. Remember, I never even saw his face. Our chances are already slim. I can't make a fool of myself. I've already gone through enough as it is."

Keith places his hands on his wife's face and reassures her, "I love you, Cassandra. You didn't deserve what this guy did to you. He has to pay. Maybe if I discreetly snoop around a little bit I'll find something."

That is just what Keith does. He goes into the Bush's Sport Bar wearing dark sunglasses. Keith takes them off after a while. He makes very little contact with anybody, but he is watching very closely—more than anybody realizes. Sitting at the bar, Keith orders a martini just to appear occupied. He pays close attention to name badges. The bartender's name is Kirk, so Keith does not bother talking to him too much. This isn't the guy he is looking for. After about 30 minutes, Keith has pretty much scoped out the place but has not been able to see who Todd is.

As he rises up to leave the bar, he overhears one of the waitresses say, "Todd, James wants you to see him in the office before you start your shift."

Keith sits back down on the bar stool and sips a little of his martini. He is really waiting to see what Todd looks like. Moments later, Todd exchanges places with Kirk at the bar. Keith gets a real good look at him. He is a tall, slender but somewhat muscular young man with a light brown complexion, thick eyebrows, and hazel eyes. Todd's look is very serious in nature. He does not smile much and carries a rather rigid approach as long as no one is talking to him.

Keith initiates a conversation with him to sort of feel him out. Todd slightly grins and says, "You want another martini?"

Keith replies, "No, I'm cool... This is my first time in this place. There are a lot of girls in here. I haven't even been here one hour, and already three chicks have tried to pick me up. What's it like to work with so many pretty girls? I'm sure it's a real perk, right?" Keith only talks like this to convince Todd that he is a regular lady's man. He wants Todd to open up to him and maybe slip something out without realizing it.

Todd expounds on Keith's question, "Perk? Not anymore."

"What does that mean?" Keith asks.

"I've already dated some of these girls in here. They're old news, man, old news. I get bored real quick."

"Yeah, I know what you mean, man. So what's your type?" Keith inquires.

"All kinds, I guess. Some of them act as if they're all that, but when I get to know them, they're no better than anybody else. I hate to be with girls like that."

Momentarily Keith excuses himself. He goes into the bathroom and sets up a small cassette recorder in his jacket pocket. He wants to record Todd's voice on tape. When he returns from the bathroom, Todd is socializing with a lady at the bar. She is obviously older than Todd, at least in her early thirties. He flirts a little bit with smiles and winks and then gives her a free drink. "It's on the house," he tells her.

Keith returns to the bar and tells Todd, "I think I'll take you up on that next martini."

Todd turns around and says, "Okay. Coming right up." As Todd makes the martini, he converses with Keith. "So have you seen anybody that caught your eye yet? In this place, women just fall in your lap. You shouldn't have to look too hard. I'll bet before the night is over, you'll find at least two of them. You'll probably have to pick one." Todd starts to laugh.

Keith shares the laugh and replies, "Probably... So what was up with the one that just left the bar with the drink?"

"Oh, she was hot, wasn't she? Those are the ones to go after right there," Todd explains. "She's a little older than most girls that come in here. That type of woman seems to be a little more conservative, but she wants it just as much as the younger women do."

"Wants what?" Keith asks.

"What else? You know what I mean. They pretend not to be freaky, but they are... A few months ago, I had an experience with an older woman. She was beautiful, just great to look at. I liked looking at her. Her skin was sort of light in complexion."

"Oh yeah?" Keith replies.

"Her hair was long and wavy textured."

Cassandra's hair is long and wavy textured, and her complexion is light brown.

Todd continues, "She had a mole on her cheek. She was dressed real nice and businesslike every time I'd see her."

"Oh, so it was somebody you'd seen more than once?"

"Yeah, I would always see her around town. It was like a coincidence. Anyway, I just figured that I had to go after her. I had to be kind of aggressive with that one, though, because she pretended that she didn't want me, but I knew she did."

"What makes you think she wanted you?" Keith wonders.

"Because they always do. Even the married ones like her always want some action. She kept telling me that she had a husband. That doesn't mean anything. Mostly every woman in this place has a man at home, but they still come here."

Without realizing it, Todd is incriminating himself because Keith's tape recorder is running full speed. Todd continues to ramble on about this mysterious woman that appeared to be resistant. In his mind, she wanted to be with him. Before long he starts to spew out details—too many details.

"What was this chick's name?" Keith asks. "I need her phone number."

Todd laughs and says, "No, she's long gone. Her name was Cassandra. I could never forget that name... That's my mother's name, too."

Keith asks, "You said that this Cassandra resisted you?"

Todd answers, "Yeah, she put up a fight, but I just kept going. I gave her what she really wanted even though she pretended not to want it."

After a few minutes, Keith politely ends the conversation. "I better go now. I have to pull a night shift. It was nice talking to you—Todd. I like this place. Maybe I'll check it out again sometime. Catch you later, man."

Todd nods his head and continues to assist some other customers at the bar. Before leaving, Keith takes one more look back at Todd. He then exits the bar and gets into his car. As he drives away, Keith rewinds the tape and plays it back. The clarity is excellent. There is not one word muffled or inaudible on the tape. He takes it home and lets Cassandra listen to it.

Immediately upon hearing Todd's voice on the tape, Cassandra reacts. "I'm getting chill bumps just listening to him, Keith... That's him, definitely him."

"This is only the beginning, baby. Do you know that I sat down for almost an hour with this guy, and all he talked about was girls and how they always want sex but pretend not to want it? He alluded to several things."

"Did you get any specifics about me?"

Keith continues to play the tape. Todd describes Cassandra physically and even states her name. He is also descriptive about a few things that she could corroborate in her own account, such as the neck kissing. In addition, on the tape Todd is heard stating that he went over the top with this one and that he had a lot to drink that night. Keith recalls his wife initially telling him that her rapist's breath smelled like beer. As Cassandra continues to listen to the tape, she shakes her head and states, "I can't believe this guy. He actually thought that I wanted to be there with him? I fought him tooth and nail."

Keith explains, "In his mind, your resistance was just a cover-up. He honestly felt that you were signaling him to pursue you further. In other words, to him your no meant yes. Apparently he has seen you on more than one occasion. He's been watching you."

"Yeah, he told me that too. He said that he could always tell when I was here alone in the house. That's real creepy."

Keith and Cassandra present their evidence to the police. Sergeant Murphy compliments Keith's work and says, "I have to hand it to you, Mr. Glover. You threw out the bait, and you caught a big fish."

"My wife was concerned about not getting a good look at his face."

"Well, that is a factor to consider. However, the tape coincides with her initial story. There are certain details that he stated that just could not be coincidental. We at least have enough to bring him in for questioning. It's a start. If he can't come up with a totally good alibi for where he was that night during the incident, then he may have some trouble on his hands."

Todd Lincoln is brought in to the police station for questioning. "I'm telling you people that you have the wrong guy! I didn't rape no lady! I was at work!"

Sergeant Murphy replies, "Some of your co-workers told us that you left work at about 9:45

after having a few drinks. The incident occurred roughly between 10 o'clock and 10:30 that night. That allows fifteen to forty-five minutes for you to gain contact with the victim. Now unless you can come up with a good alibi to cover that time period, then I suggest you start talking truth!"

"I didn't do it!" Todd angrily defends. Just then, he catches a glimpse of Cassandra at the water fountain down the hallway. She deliberately wants him to see her so that it can be observed how he reacts to her presence. Todd stares for a moment, then he looks away.

"Is there something wrong, Mr. Lincoln?" Sergeant Van Horn asks.

Todd appears to be uneasy as he slightly changes his seated position and slouches somewhat in the shoulders. It is obvious that he reacted to seeing his victim. Nonetheless, he still tries to remain calm and well controlled. This changes when Sergeant Van Horn says, "I have something that I want you to hear, Mr. Lincoln." She places the cassette recorder on the table in front of him and begins to play the tape. Todd's face turns flush red as he realizes that he has been set up. As the tape continues to play, Sergeant Murphy asks Keith to proceed forward.

"Mr. Lincoln, have you ever seen this man before?" Sergeant Murphy asks.

Todd looks away and demands, "I want my lawyer. Get me a lawyer."

Keith stares him down until Todd shouts, "Would you make him leave me alone? Tell him to stop doing that!" He is intimidated by Keith's staring.

Keith tightens his fists as Cassandra quickly steps in front of him, "No! No, baby, he's not worth it!" She grabs hold of her husband's hands and restrains him.

Keith angrily stares at Todd as tears stream down his face. His jaw flinches, as he is ready to attack Todd. Suddenly, Keith raises his hands in front of himself and tells his wife, "I'm okay." Keith walks away.

Cassandra focuses on Todd Lincoln for a moment. Then she asks him, "Was it worth it? Think about what you did to me. Was it worth it?" He does not look at her or answer her question. Cassandra walks away.

Keith is outside leaning up against the car with his arms folded. He is staring down at the ground but looks up when he notices Cassandra joining him outside. He reaches out for her and gives her a warm embrace. "I love you. You're the most important person in this world to me, Cassandra… I almost snapped in there. I almost shoved my fist right into his mouth."

"He's not worth it, baby. You conquered your anger, and that's a good thing. I'm proud of what you've done. You got right up in his face and made him tell on himself. You did all of that for me… Thank you."

Keith kisses his wife and continues to hold her in his arms. "I'd do anything for you. You know that."

She smiles and lovingly places her arms around him, giving Keith a big squeeze. "I love you, Keith."

Todd Lincoln is sentenced to five years in prison coupled with psychiatric evaluations. He is a 25-year-old bartender who formerly lived with his mother. When asked why he committed this sex crime, Todd Lincoln replies, "It felt good to be in charge... It felt good to make somebody do what I wanted them to do."

Cassandra puts her life back together piece by piece. Her relief comes from knowing that Todd Lincoln is in prison where he belongs. Also, she knows that Keith is a loving, supportive husband who will always be right by her side. She has confidence in him.

Keith receives a phone call from his previous job. "Baby, they want me to come back."

Cassandra replies, "They do?"

"Yeah, that was Bob Morgan. He wants to speak with me tomorrow and negotiate a little bit."

Bob Morgan is CEO of the factory where Keith had worked before being laid off. He humbly admits that the layoff was a big mistake and asks Keith to come back with higher pay than when he left. "Your pay will be considerably higher, Keith. I discussed the salary offer with Harold Price, and we mutually agreed on $18 an hour with the opportunity for bonuses and another raise after six months."

Keith used to make $14 an hour.

"On a personal level, I just want you to know that I voted against the layoffs. I had nothing to do personally with what happened to you and those other people. Keith, I like you and have always admired your work ethic. I was outnumbered by a committee. I'm sorry that this happened to you."

Keith replies, "I understand, Mr. Morgan. I don't blame you in particular. I could always tell that you really cared about the people who work here."

"When can you start again?"

"Well, I believe that it would be fair to give two weeks' notice to my current supervisor."

"Very well, then. I look forward to seeing you in the first week of next month. Welcome back, Keith." Bob Morgan shakes Keith's hand and escorts him out of his office. "Have a good day, Keith."

"You too, Mr. Morgan."

As Keith is about to step into the elevator, one of his former co-workers sees him. Anthony Peterson is a 29-year-old truck driver for the company. He is loading some packages onto his truck and has just come back inside to refuel his energy with a quick snack. "Hey, Keith, how are you doing, man? It's good to see you."

"Likewise."

"Are you coming back?" Anthony asks.

"It appears to be that way. I start again at the beginning of next month."

"You see that? I knew they couldn't do it without you. You were an asset to this factory. They asked you back because they realized that they needed you."

"I'll catch you later, Anthony. Good to see you."

"Bye, Keith. Take care."

Meanwhile, Mrs. Glover misses Mr. Sanders terribly. She loves him very much and has been tempted many times to reconcile with him. One Sunday morning, she is in the front yard watering her garden when she experiences a sharp, gnawing pain in her side. Mrs. Glover grimaces in pain and drops her water hose. She goes inside the house and takes some pain medication and rests on the sofa for a while until the pain gradually subsides.

These pain symptoms become recurrent in nature, but Mrs. Glover neglects to see her doctor. The great amount of stress over a period of time has gradually caused her to develop a peptic ulcer in her stomach; nevertheless, she does not realize this at first.

The following Sunday evening while the family is having dinner, Mrs. Glover begins to feel a burning sensation in her stomach, again associated with sharp pain. Keith and Cassandra can tell that something is wrong even though Mrs. Glover does not mention her problem.

"Mama, are you alright?" Keith asks. "You seem troubled."

"Oh, I've just been having these sharp pains in my stomach."

"For how long?" Cassandra inquires.

"Since the last week or so."

"You may need to see your doctor," Cassandra recommends.

"Oh, I just take a couple of pain pills, and it goes away," Mrs. Glover reasons.

"Yeah, but if it keeps happening, then there could be something wrong." Cassandra adds.

Keith intervenes, "Mama, make an appointment with your doctor."

Mrs. Glover's primary care physician, Dr. Caleb Morris, prescribes a medication to treat the ulcer. "Make sure you take these pills, Mrs. Glover. It's very important that you do this."

When Mrs. Glover returns home, she informs the family that she has a stress-related ulcer. Everyone grows worried.

Keith tells her, "You see, Mama, I knew something had to be wrong. You were trying to self-medicate with aspirin and not tell us about this. That bothers me. You weren't going to even see your doctor until we prompted you to."

Mrs. Glover defends, "I've always been as healthy as a horse."

"Mama, lately you've been so depressed and stressed out. So much has happened lately. You've been pulled in every direction, and now it's time for you to take it easy for a while. Let us help you."

Mrs. Glover is used to being very independent. She never asks anyone to do much for her, but now Keith insists that his mother slow down due to her health issues. Every day now, she spends much of her time inside the house lying in bed and sinking lower into a state of depression. Stephanie, Keith, and Cassandra wait on her hand and foot, trying to make sure that their mother does not worsen her condition by over-extending herself.

The family receives some disturbing news from one of their relatives in Texas. At the time of the phone call, Keith is visiting his mother to make sure that she is taking her medication and resting.

"Hello, Uncle Jarvis."

"Hello Keith, how are you?" It sounds as if Jarvis is upset.

"Uncle Jarvis, are you alright?" Keith inquires.

Mrs. Glover's older sister Doris is married to Jarvis Singh. Jarvis is weeping because Doris has passed away. She and Mrs. Glover have not spoken in two years. They had a disagreement over the phone one day, and neither of them put forth the effort to contact the other one again. As time passed, the distance grew between the once-close siblings. It appears that Doris succumbed to a stroke.

Keith feels terrible about losing his aunt; however, he is also wondering how he is going to break the news to his mother in her delicate condition.

When he gets off the phone with Doris's husband, Keith sighs as he rests his hand over his forehead. He shakes his head and mumbles to himself, "I don't believe this."

"Believe what?" Mrs. Glover asks. Keith did not realize that she was standing there. He is alarmed by her presence.

"Mama, I thought you were lying down."

"Who was that?"

"Uncle Jarvis," Keith replies. He regrets having to tell his mother that her estranged sister has passed away.

"Oh, well, what did he say? Did Doris come to the phone?"

"No Mama, she didn't."

"Well, why would Jarvis call me and not have Doris come to the phone? Keith, what's going on? I guess she's still punishing me."

Keith sighs and asks his mother to sit down. Mrs. Glover stubbornly remains standing. "Keith, what is it?"

"Please sit down," he politely asks again.

Mrs. Glover continues to stand and demands that her son explain to her what is going on.

"Mama, Uncle Jarvis called to tell you that Doris suffered from a stroke."

"Oh, my goodness. Is she alright?"

Keith lowers his head and shakes his head no.

Mrs. Glover knows exactly what this means and stands in her tracks momentarily. She is in shock.

"Mama, Mama, I'm sorry."

"Well I'll be. Jarvis says that Doris is gone." Mrs. Glover makes a transition from shock to denial. "There's no way that Doris could be dead. She's too stubborn to die."

Keith reiterates, "She's gone, Mama."

"No!" Mrs. Glover shouts. She is becoming upset and begins to vent. "How could you do this, Doris? How could you just walk off the face of the earth like this without saying goodbye to me? How could you? We never got to talk, Doris. We never got to talk." Mrs. Glover begins to weep bitterly. "I loved you Doris—with all my heart. I'm so sorry for what I said to make you mad. You always told me that I had to be right all the time and that I didn't listen to you."

Keith rises up and consoles his mother. She continues speaking. "Keith, she never called me. She never called me again. Maybe Doris didn't love me anymore."

"Yes she did, Mama. She was just stubborn, that's all."

"Two years! Two years went by, and I didn't even get to say goodbye to her, Keith!" Mrs. Glover embraces her son as he comforts her.

"It's going to be alright, Mama. We're going to get through this."

Mrs. Glover expresses, "First your brother leaves and doesn't come back, then Bartholomew and I don't get married, and now Doris is dead! I'm so tired, Keith. I'm so tired of suffering! I feel like my life is falling apart. Every time I make two steps forward, I get set back three steps."

"Come on, Mama, lie down on the sofa. Just lie down, okay?" Keith assists his mother to the sofa.

For several days, she weeps bitterly over her sister's death. Mrs. Glover is overwhelmed with a sense of loss that started with Gerard. She fears that he has gotten back into his old habits and gotten into trouble or even been murdered. It hurts her to know that he may never come back. There are also feelings of guilt that keep resurfacing. Not having her son around has broken Mrs. Glover's spirit. She is crushed.

Keith pays Mr. Sanders a visit. "Keith, what a surprise. Please, come in."

"Thank you," Keith says as he enters Mr. Sanders' home.

"Have a seat Keith... So, what brings you by here? How's your mother?"

"Unfortunately, she's had a setback. Her sister died a few days ago. She's really distressed over it."

"I'm sorry to hear that, Keith... I'd like to see your mother, if she's up for my company. In fact, there isn't a day that goes by that I don't think of her. I love Marguerite very much, and I did want to make her happy. I've been suffering, too. It's just not the same without her."

"She misses you, Mr. Sanders. She doesn't say it, but I know that you not being around has taken its toll on her. In fact, my mother has an ulcer. Her doctor placed her on medication."

Mr. Sanders is deeply concerned. "I must see her," he insists.

Mrs. Glover's eyes are puffy and red due to excessive crying. She is deeply saddened over her recent experiences. When Mr. Sanders visits her, she expresses delight in seeing him despite her condition. "Bartholomew, I'm happy to see you... I thought you had forgotten about me."

Mr. Sanders replies, "Of course not, dear. Of course not. I love you, Marguerite. I could never forget you or what we shared. It means too much to me to forget."

"My sister died."

"Yes, Keith told me."

"He did?"

"Yes, he visited me and told me. I'm sorry about your sister."

"We used to be so close. However, two years ago, something happened between us that changed our relationship. We had a disagreement over something that means nothing now, and for the last two years we haven't spoken. I'm so mad at myself, Bartholomew. I wasn't even angry with Doris anymore, but I still didn't pick up that phone and just call her. She didn't call me either. She took that stubbornness to the grave, and now I'm sitting here wishing that I had just picked up the phone and been humble enough to apologize. Who was right or wrong doesn't really matter."

"Don't be so hard on yourself, Marguerite. I'm sure that your sister knew that you loved her, and she loved you. You have to believe that."

"I didn't even get to say goodbye. She's gone."

Mr. Sanders continues to sit with Mrs. Glover. He offers to make her some tea. She accepts. "The tea cups are in the top cabinet on the far left."

When Mr. Sanders makes the tea, he sets it in front of Mrs. Glover on the table and continues to talk to her. "I remembered, two sugars, right?"

Mrs. Glover nods, "Umm-hmm, two sugars." She sips her tea and asks, "Bartholomew, how are your children doing?"

"Well, Marvin and Angela are doing well. Carlton and I are still not speaking."

"You must reconcile with him. Don't be like Doris and me."

"I love my son, but he's hot-headed and stubborn... His wife left him."

"She did?"

"Yes, Katrina left. She told Carlton that unless he sought some counseling that she wasn't going to be with him."

"Let me guess—he refused the counseling," Mrs. Glover assumes.

Mr. Sanders confirms, "Yes, he refused to do it. Now Katrina and Dimitri are living with her mother, at least temporarily. To add to all of this, she's pregnant. Somehow they managed to find time for this despite their problems. I don't know what they're going to do. I would hate to see Dimitri and the new baby suffer on account of their parents' differences. I totally blame my son for this. He has a good wife who loves him, but he's just pushed her to the limit now."

"Well, I hope that things work out for Carlton and Katrina."

"Marguerite, I need to be with you. I don't just 'want' to be with you. I need to be. I love you very much, and ever since you broke off the engagement I've been a mess. Not a day goes by that I don't think of you."

"Bartholomew, I just didn't feel right marrying you after Carlton gave you such an ultimatum. I never wanted things to be like that."

"It wasn't your fault, though. I kept telling you that. Marguerite, what Carlton did was wrong. Of course I didn't want to lose my son, but he put me in a position to choose. He did that, not you. Besides, no matter how much I love my children, I love you too. I wasn't going to give up on you. I had already made that determination, and I still want to marry you. I love you."

"I've missed you, Bartholomew."

Mrs. Glover and Mr. Sanders decide to get married, and this time they are not turning back.

Mrs. Glover plans to attend her sister's memorial service. Keith, Cassandra, their children,

Stephanie and her family, Robbie, and Mr. Sanders accompany her to Texas. She is still not completely well but forces herself to make the trip. It is difficult for her, but her children prove to be a source of encouragement. They love her dearly. Mr. Sanders is a great help as well.

There are moments when Mrs. Glover remains silent while everyone else converses. Keith understands that his mother is probably sad that Gerard is not around. He knows that his mother misses his brother terribly. When the family returns home from Texas, Keith decides to secretly search for his brother, not only for his mother's sake but also for his own sanity. As hard as it is for Keith to admit it, he worries about Gerard and wonders where he is and what he's doing. He seeks out some of Gerard's old buddies that he himself knew on a personal level. No one has heard from Gerard.

The night before her wedding, Mrs. Glover wakes up from a horrible nightmare about Gerard. In the dream, she is reaching for his hand as he screams out to her for help. He is falling down a dark hole, and his mother is trying to no avail to rescue him. The dream frightens Mrs. Glover and causes her to breathe with difficulty. Her heart is racing.

She cannot sleep now, so Mrs. Glover goes into her kitchen and drinks a glass of water. Before returning to bed, she enters her den and sits down on the sofa. Mrs. Glover starts to look through some of her old photo albums of her children when they were young. She giggles as she comes across a picture of Keith looking handsome with his afro and mustache. At the time, he was a high school senior. There is also a picture of him and Gerard affectionately standing with their arms around each other. They must have been between ages 10 and 13. Reminiscing helps Mrs. Glover feel somewhat better, and she returns to bed. She realizes that she was just dreaming.

The next afternoon, Mrs. Glover and Mr. Sanders are accompanied by their respective children to the local courthouse.

"Do you, Bartholomew James Sanders, take Marguerite Elaine Glover to be your lawfully wedded wife—"

"I do," Mr. Sanders eagerly states before Judge Anthony Smith can even finish speaking.

The judge slightly grins and says, "You're in quite a hurry aren't you?" He is teasing Mr. Sanders. The audience finds this to be humorous as Mr. Sanders blushes. He and Mrs. Glover share a laugh.

After the ceremony, the two families meet back at Marvin's home to celebrate. Carlton did not show up at the courthouse for the event; however, he arrives at his brother's house. At first everyone feels a little awkward with him being there; nonetheless, his sister Angela breaks the ice by greeting him with a hello and a pat on the back.

"Carlton, how are you?"

"Okay." He is somewhat nervous but manages to approach his father and apologize.

Mr. Sanders accepts and lovingly embraces his son. "Carlton, there's just one more thing that I want you to do. I want you to apologize to Marguerite as well."

Mrs. Glover intervenes, "No, Bartholomew, it's alright."

"No, it isn't alright. I was wrong for what I did. I came between you and my father, and I was wrong for that. Will you please forgive me?" Carlton begs.

Mrs. Glover nods her head and reaches out to hug her new stepson. Robbie looks on in silence as he sips a drink. As Robbie turns away, Carlton speaks to him. "Robbie, there's no excuse for what I did to you that day. I was way out of line. Can you find it in your heart to forgive me? I'm really sorry, man."

139

Robbie still does not feel completely good about his new stepbrother; however, for his mother's sake, Robbie reconciles with Carlton. His wife Katrina sends their son Dimitri to Marvin's house, but she does not attend.

Just then, Angela announces, "Okay, happy couple, I hope you're hungry. Beverly and I slaved over a hot stove to make all of this stuff."

The family enjoys a buffet-style dinner and a cake for dessert. After a while, Mrs. Glover-Sanders notices that Keith is not present.

"Cassandra, where is Keith?"

"Oh, he had to stop and get something. He'll be back soon."

When Keith returns, he tells his mother, "Mama, I have something special for you."

Mrs. Glover-Sanders is expecting a gift, but Keith enters the house accompanied by Gerard. Keith had found him.

Their mother cannot believe her eyes. Mrs. Glover-Sanders is overjoyed and bursts into tears. She reaches out and embraces her long-lost son, kissing him tenderly on his face. Gerard starts to cry, "I'm so glad to see you, Mama."

"Where have you been?" she questions. "I was worried sick about you."

"Keith told me, and I'm so sorry that I put you through so much. I don't want you to be getting ulcers and worrying yourself over me. I promise, I'll never leave you again. I didn't come back sooner because you seemed fed up with me."

Keith adds, "He was living at a shelter for a while, but then he left there and moved in with an old friend who was kind enough to take him in."

Mrs. Glover-Sanders just stands there for a moment gazing up at her son. "Gerard, I'm so sorry."

"For what?" he wonders.

"For what I said to you. I didn't mean all of that stuff I said. I was just angry at the time. I don't agree with everything that you've done in your life, but you're still my son and I love you. That will never change. I think that you deserve another chance. This time you seem sincere."

"You've given me so many chances already."

"Well, I'm just not ready to give up on you yet," Mrs. Glover-Sanders replies. Once again, she embraces her son. She is so happy to see Gerard.

Gerard smiles at his mother and reassures her, "I love you. You're the best mother anyone could ever have. Once I get myself together, you're going to be so proud of me. I won't slip up this time."

Mrs. Glover and Gerard spend some time talking to each other. Keith is happy to have found his brother. Eventually, they too have an opportunity to reconcile.

One afternoon, Keith and Gerard have lunch together. "I appreciate what you did, man."

Keith replies, "Well, Gerard, the family missed you a lot. Mama was sad, and we hated seeing her that way. We all missed you though— not just her. I remember how mad I was at you when you went back to jail. I was disappointed because I had started believing in you. When you got into trouble again, it hurt me. I've always wanted better for you than what you were giving yourself. No matter what I did, you just wouldn't listen."

"Keith, I'm sorry, man. I love you."

Keith smiles at his brother and nods his head, "That's good to know. We've certainly had our share of arguments. I never thought I'd see the day when we'd be sitting here like this talking… Just stay on the right track this time. You owe it to yourself. I'm only saying this because I care about you. I always did love you, Gerard, even when I was being hard on you. I was just trying to help you. That's all."

Gerard acknowledges, "I realize that."

Keith takes something out of his pocket. "Remember this?" He shows him the picture of them when they were children embracing one another.

Gerard looks at the picture and says, "We were best friends, man. I looked out for you, and you looked out for me. Let's start over right now."

Keith and Gerard overcome their differences and become friends again—not just brothers. It takes some time to put things back together again, but eventually it happens.

So far Robbie has not really put much effort into bonding with Gerard. He went back to California a few days after his mother's wedding ceremony. However, he decides to call his brother.

"Gerard, it's Robbie."

Gerard assumes that his brother wants to speak with their mother, but Robbie surprises him.

"I called for you especially… We haven't talked."

"No, we haven't, man. So what's up?"

"Gerard, I know that we've had our share of problems, but you're still my brother. I worried about you just like everybody else did. I just thought you should know that. When we were kids, I looked up to you. I was also grateful when you would stand up for me and keep all of those bullies away from me. Do you remember that time when Alfred Johnson was going to beat me up, and you came to scare him off? It was so funny how you chased him down the street and had him crying like a girl."

"Hey, I had to protect my little brother."

For a moment, there is silence. Then Robbie utters, "So what are you doing these days?"

"Well, our new stepbrother Marvin made some contacts for me and got me a job. I'm working for one of his friends at a construction site."

"Good, very good. Just hang in there."

"I will. I've spent my whole life doing nothing, and I can't continue down that road. I can't get back what I've lost, but I can use what I have."

"Well, you can call me anytime if you want to talk. If you need anything, I'll help you."

"Robbie, I appreciate that. Thank you."

Gerard is relieved to have had this conversation with Robbie. They have made peace with each other.

Initially, Mr. Sanders wanted to sell or rent his home when he and Mrs. Glover got married. He offers to let Gerard stay in the house. Since the home is paid for, Gerard responsibly covers the utilities and the maintenance. He keeps working at the construction company and never returns to street life again. He has turned over a new leaf. Unfortunately, he loses Teresa forever. By the time he tries to contact her, she has moved away. Despite this, Gerard feels good to have loved someone and to be loved in return. He knew that Teresa really did see something special in him. Even though brief, the time that he and Teresa shared was priceless. He hopes that wherever she is, Teresa will find someone worthy of her.

Keith continues to work for the factory again. His oldest daughter Chavonne graduates high school and attends college on a full scholarship. Her major is business communications. Keith's wife Cassandra continues to work as a claims adjuster for an insurance company. She gets promoted to branch manager when the former manager resigns.

Stephanie and her husband Jason bring their relationship back to life, so to speak. In fact, Jason tries very hard to keep things in perspective and even sells his portion of one of his businesses so that he can have less to worry about and spend more quality time with his family. He is more romantic and tells Stephanie that he loves her every day. This is music to her ears.

Robbie continues to practice law in California. After a few years, however, he sells his beach property and moves back home. He is now a partner of the Law Office of Adler, Glover & Schultz.

Carlton and Katrina Sanders both agree to seek counseling in order to work on their marriage. In addition to the couple sessions, Dr. Leslie Norman recommends that Carlton undergo anger management therapy. He agrees to this arrangement and says that he will do anything it takes to get his wife to come back home.

Even though Carlton starts to show signs of improvement, Katrina is not quick to take him back right away. In fact, it takes close to a year for her to finally reconcile with her husband and move back home. She firmly makes it clear that the first slip-up will cost them their marriage for good. As a result, Carlton humbly walks on a tight rope and makes sure that he does nothing to cause more friction or violence between the couple. Katrina gives birth to a beautiful baby girl, Nyla.

Mr. and Mrs. Bartholomew Sanders are as happy as ever as they embark upon their marriage. They both are glad to have found someone to spend their lives with after being alone for so long.

Mrs. Marguerite Glover-Sanders continues to watch her health and tries not to get too stressed out since she has an ulcer. Medication and plenty of rest help to alleviate the symptoms, in addition to a good dose of love and companionship. Every morning now, both she and Mr. Sanders walk their dog Max. Sometimes they pass Mr. Sanders's former home and stop to talk to Gerard.

Mrs. Marguerite Glover-Sanders continues to maintain a close bond with her adult children. They will always need her no matter what. She reminds them constantly that she needs them too. After all, they are the ones that she holds dear to her heart…

ABOUT THE AUTHOR

Charvella J. Campbell is a northern Florida native who currently resides in Fort Lauderdale, Florida, with her husband and two children.

Most of her time is spent with her family; however, Charvella also continues to write poetry and short stories. Her other hobbies include singing, playing tennis, and art.

Even though her work is fiction-based with no reference to any particular person(s), Charvella often draws upon on her own personal experiences and other observations for material when writing. The author describes herself as a writer who truly feels the depths of her characters and makes them come alive. Charvella uses a simple, everyday writing style with the objective of reaching her reader's mind and heart, hoping that the person will gain something valuable from her work.

Charvella is always open for comments from her readers and can be contacted via email at **CharvellaCampbell@comcast.net**.

Printed in the United States
1418600001B/211-219